How Could You Do This To Me, MUM?

How Could You Do This To Me, Mum?

ROSIE RUSHTON

Piccadilly Press • London

For Margie and Richard with love

First published in 1996
by Piccadilly Press Ltd, 5 Castle Road,
London NW1 8PR

This edition published 2006

A catalogue record of this book is available from the British Library

ISBN: 1 85340 843 3 (trade paperback)
EAN: 978 185340 408434

1 3 5 7 9 10 8 6 4 2

Printed and bound in Great Britain by Bookmarque Ltd
Typeset by M Rules, London
Cover design by Sue Hellard and Simon Davis
Set in Bembo, Courier and GilliansHand

www.piccadillypress.co.uk

Chapter One

Ring In the New!

NEW YEAR RESOLUTIONS

1. I resolve not to think about Jon Joseph ever again.
2. I resolve to stop biting my fingernails.
3. I resolve to finish writing my novel.

Signed

Laura A. Turnbull

Laura gazed at her list of New Year resolutions and picked up her pen. She'd have to squeeze in another one – the most important.

4. I resolve to help put an end to the persecution of our planet, the atrocities against animal life and the waste of our natural resources.

She surveyed the last sentence with satisfaction. It had a nice ring to it, as befitted one who, in the not too distant future, would be hailed as the new literary sensation of her age.

From now on, she told herself, pinning the amended list back on the cork tile that served as her noticeboard, life was going to be different. Daniel had made her see the light.

As she rummaged through her chest of drawers in search of her games kit, she thought about Daniel Browning, who lived next door to them in their new house in Berrydale. He had turned up on the doorstep on Boxing Day, proffering an invitation for them all to go to his parents' Punch and Pickings party on New Year's Eve. Normally Laura wouldn't have been seen dead going out socially with her mum and Melvyn, but she decided that by going next door she wouldn't have to spend the evening at The Stomping Ground with the others. Jemma, who was head over heels in love with Rob, had told her that Jon had invited Sumitha, and Chelsea had talked of nothing but the Gorgeous Guy ever since he'd arrived to stay with the Gees on Christmas Eve. The thing Laura couldn't bear was the thought of being the only one there without a boyfriend. And Daniel did have a bum to die for.

Stuffing her games socks into her kit bag, she thought back to the party. Halfway through the evening, when the parents had reached that silly stage that follows four glasses of rum punch, Laura had escaped the humiliation of watching Melvyn doing his Elton John impression by fleeing to the kitchen where the buffet was laid out and pinching a couple of chicken tikka bites.

'You're not actually going to eat those, are you?' Daniel

had demanded, appearing at her elbow with a dish of vegetable samosas.

'Pardon?' she had replied.

'Meat,' Daniel had hissed. 'Don't you know what happens to battery hens? Come with me.'

He had dragged her off to his den, and that was when she saw the posters. Everywhere. Animal Aid, Save The Whale, Protect Our Forests, Compassion In World Farming – all over the walls.

He had grabbed a pile of leaflets and thrust them into her hands: horrible pictures of chickens cooped up by the dozen in tiny, dark cages, pigs being artificially fattened and calves tethered so tightly they couldn't move their necks.

Laura had gulped. 'I know, it's awful,' she'd admitted. 'But then, me giving up meat won't make any difference, will it?' Laura was very partial to her food.

Daniel had slammed his fist on the desk top.

'It's because too many people take that attitude that these sort of atrocities are allowed to go on! It just makes me so angry . . .'

'What's that?' Laura had interrupted, pointing to the corner of the room where a large piece of cardboard was stuck on top of a broom handle.

'It's supposed to be a placard for a demo outside Leehampton Research Labs in a couple of weeks,' he had said. 'They use animals for all sorts of terrible tests – squirting shampoo in their eyes and stuff. Only I can't think of anything snappy to write on it,' he'd added dolefully.

Laura had closed her eyes, screwed up her nose and thought.

'How about, *Do you really want looks an animal has died for,*' she'd suggested. 'You know, a play on she's got looks to die for?'

'That's brilliant!' he'd said admiringly. 'Hey, why don't you come along to the demo? We can do with all the support we can get.'

I might just go, thought Laura, hurling a crumpled netball skirt to the floor. After all, Daniel was rather cute, with that thick blond hair that had a slight wave and made you want to run your fingers through it and such velvety brown eyes. He was at Sixth Form college doing resits, which would be one up on having a boyfriend still at school. At least by being out on a Saturday morning her mother wouldn't be able to persuade her to go on the inevitable shopping trip to Mothercare. She needed some compensation for having a mother who was getting to look more like a hippo every day, and spent her time reading leaflets on breastfeeding and going ga-ga over mobiles of fluffy lambs. She remembered Daniel's remark at the party.

'Your mum – I mean, she's not preggers, is she?' he had said.

'Mmm,' Laura had murmured, pulling a face. 'It's due in March.'

'Woah!' Daniel had said. 'She's a bit old for that sort of stuff, isn't she? Is your dad pleased?'

'Melvyn's not my dad.'

'Oh, second marriage?' Daniel had asked.

'No, they're not married, they just live together.'

Daniel had pulled a face.

'So what's wrong with that? And anyway, they're getting married soon,' Laura had snapped.

'OK, OK, keep your hair on.' Daniel had laughed gently. 'I'm not fussed either way. Except, of course, that we could do without people adding to the population explosion, married or not.' He'd taken a swig of cider. 'Mind you, if the new baby has your looks, it will be a stunner,' he'd added, grinning at her.

Remembering the compliment, Laura sighed. Jon had never called her a stunner. Stop it, she admonished herself severely. Remember Resolution Number One. Jon is history. Jon is finished with. So why did she keep thinking about him? Why, every morning for the first week of term, had she peered out of the school bus in the hope of catching sight of him? And when she had spotted him, why had her stomach lurched uncontrollably?

Well, from now on she would turn her attention to something really worthwhile. Laura Turnbull would start saving the planet.

Chapter Two

Chelsea Does Some Star-Gazing

Over in Thorburn Crescent, Chelsea Gee's thoughts were on a lesser plane. She was sprawled out on the bed, trying to sort out her own private world with the help of *Yell!* magazine's Stars for the New Year supplement.

PSYCHIC SANDY REVEALS WHAT'S IN YOUR
STARS THIS NEW YEAR
AQUARIUS (21 January – 19 February)

You're feeling a bit hard done by right now but don't despair; life cannot always be one long party and things will hot up again soon as you make new friends and share new experiences. In fact, this could be your year! But be sure not to bite off more than you can chew; not everything is what it seems. In the meantime, count your blessings and remember you're surrounded by people who love you – so shake off those doldrums and be happy!

'So what does she know?' mumbled Chelsea, hurling the magazine across the room. She knew she should be getting her kit ready for school and finishing her French assignment, but since whatever she did these days was bound to go wrong, she had decided not to bother doing anything at all.

Life, she thought, was the pits. It was all very well for Psychic Sandy to say count your blessings, but she wasn't a practically-fifteen-year-old whose parents had not only said they couldn't afford to buy her an iPod for her birthday but had even refused to let her have a party. They said it was because they'd only just had Christmas and money was tight and she would have to be content with going out for a meal.

Not that there was much point having a party when you didn't have a boyfriend. She still got knots in her stomach thinking about how Rob had gone off with Jemma at the end of last term. He'd had the nerve to tell her she came on too strong. Just because she had a bit of verve. They were only one week into the new term and already Chelsea was sick of hearing Jemma go on about what film Rob had taken her to and how great he was before saying, 'Oh, sorry, Chelsea, I didn't mean to upset you!'

Psychic Sandy hadn't got a clue – the fact was, no one round here loved her any more. Not only had Rob deserted her, but her mum was too busy writing newspaper features and fronting this new radio phone-in show – *Live Lines to Ginny* – and having hot flushes and bad moods all over the place to take any notice of Chelsea. Except to nag, of course. She always had time for that. As for her father, he had brought further shame and ignominy on her by decorating the roof of his soup kitchen van with two giant wooden spoons on which he painted the soups of the day in lurid fluorescent letters and drove round town like some common street vendor. It wasn't as if he made loads of money; that might have made the shame slightly more bearable.

When Geneva had phoned from Mombasa on Christmas Day, the parents had been ecstatic and spent the whole afternoon saying how well she had done, and what a worker she was and wasn't she enterprising going to Africa on her own? When Warwick said that his old bike was falling to bits and he needed something to get to lectures on, they had handed him a cheque and told him to buy a new one. But when Chelsea wanted something so badly, what happened? 'Money doesn't grow on trees, Chelsea', 'Join the real world, Chelsea.' They hate me, she thought miserably.

Her life was just a joke to them. When she'd told them about the split with Rob, all her mother had said was, 'There'll be plenty more fish in the sea,' which was a pretty useless comment coming from someone who was supposed to be The Listening Mum with the Ear of the Young. And her dad had gone on about her having her whole life ahead of her and not wanting to fill her head with boy nonsense. What did they know?

Even her plans for wowing Guy, the gorgeous six foot hunk from California whom Warwick had brought home from uni for the Christmas holidays, had gone astray. When he'd asked her to show him a good time on New Year's Eve, she had thought she was home and dry, but what had happened? She'd spent hours getting ready, piling her chestnut hair on top of her head to look really sophisticated and spraying herself with this wicked new perfume, Appeal. And yet within minutes of arriving at The Stomping Ground's Free For All New Year Stampede, Guy had spotted Ella Barlow, who had the figure of a supermodel and the brain of an undernourished pea, and that was the last Chelsea had seen of him all evening.

If it hadn't been for Bex, she probably would have gone home. Bex was a year above Chelsea in school – when she was actually at school, that is. She had raven black hair cut into hedgehog spikes, loads of earrings, a nose stud and the reputation of being a rebel. None of Chelsea's crowd had anything to do with Bex or her mates, who tended to loll around with bored expressions on their faces and smoke a lot – but while Chelsea had been leaning against the wall, wishing Laura was there and trying to avoid looking at Rob slobbering all over Jemma, Bex had flopped down on the stool next to her and said, 'Trug quite fancies you,' matter of factly. 'He wants me to drag you over. Coming?'

Chelsea hadn't had a clue who Trug was, but anyone would be better than no one on a night like this, she'd thought, and had followed Bex to a corner table.

'This is Trug,' she'd said, shoving Chelsea in the direction of a gangly guy with long tangled hair and enough ironmongery in his ears to start a small steel works.

'Wanna dance?' Trug had said, jerking his head towards the dance floor.

'OK,' Chelsea had replied, casting an eye over his shoulder and noting with satisfaction that Guy was watching her closely.

'What do you do?' she'd asked as Trug wrapped his arms round her neck and began gyrating to the music. Apparently he was on the dole, played the guitar in subways and was waiting to be discovered as the latest rock sensation. Once he had informed her of that fact, he hadn't talked much but had swayed about. Chelsea decided he wasn't really her type, but perhaps just seeing her with someone else would fire Guy with unrestrained jealousy. She'd looked to where he was standing, deep in conversation with Supermodel. He hadn't appeared to be suffering much.

She had spent the rest of the evening with Bex and the gang. There had been one high spot when Jemma had come up, all smiles, hand in hand with Rob who was gazing at her adoringly, and said, 'Hi, Chelsea, great evening, isn't it?'

Chelsea, who'd felt like bursting into tears at the sight of them together, had snapped, 'I suppose you would enjoy it – any time away from Mummy's apron strings is a bonus for you, isn't it?' and had been very satisfied to see a look of admiration flash across the faces of her new-found friends. Jemma had bitten her lip and turned crimson and Rob had dragged her off, throwing a look that could have killed in Chelsea's direction. 'Mate of yours?' Bex had queried. 'Not any more,' Chelsea had muttered darkly.

Then a girl called Fee had begun talking at length about social inequality and how she reckoned her parents were a blight on society because they had two cars and stocks and shares and spent their holidays in Barbados.

'Fee,' Bex had said admiringly, 'is very socially aware. Are your lot into anything worthwhile?'

Chelsea hadn't been quite sure what the right answer would be.

'My mum works for the *Echo*,' she'd ventured, 'Dad's a . . . catering consultant.'

'She's not that Ginny Gee woman, is she?' Bex had asked. 'The one who goes on Hot FM sometimes?'

Chelsea had nodded reluctantly. Bex had looked impressed.

'Oh yawn,' Fee had droned. 'That middle class, here's how to deal with your stroppy teenagers stuff . . .'

'Yeah, so boring,' Bex had said hastily.

Out of the corner of her eye, Chelsea had seen Supermodel and Guy in a clinch. So much for making him jealous. She'd been glad that the worst of the evening was over. Or so she had thought. When the party had broken up, everyone had piled outside and Chelsea had stopped dead on the pavement in horror.

'What's the matter?' Bex had asked.

'Oh no!' Chelsea had breathed.

Parked on the opposite kerb was her dad's soup kitchen van, and there, bold as brass standing on the pavement was her father, wearing a striped butcher's apron and shouting at the top of his voice, 'Come and get your Hogmanay Hotpot here! Treat yourself to a hot start to the New Year! Come and . . . oh, hi Chelsea, ready to go?' he had shouted across the road.

'Is that your dad?' Fee and Bex had chorused in unison, smirking at one another.

'You never said he ran a soup kitchen,' sneered Trug. 'Got any handouts for the poor and needy then, mate?' he yelled across the street.

Chelsea hadn't even bothered to reply. She had just watched her reputation vanish into thin air. She had never been so embarrassed in her whole life, but her thoughts were interrupted by a shout from the object of her angst.

'Chelsea? Chelsea, come down here, please. I need your help. Now!'

She pulled a face at the closed door, picked up the magazine and went on reading. After what her father had done to her, she didn't owe him any favours.

Chapter Three

Dramatic Developments

Jemma's reading matter was giving her a great deal more pleasure than Chelsea's.

'I think, Jemma dear,' Miss Olive had said to her when she went for her assessment class on the first Saturday of term, 'I think you have considerable talent and a great deal of potential. I watched you as Nancy in *Oliver!* at your school, you know. My nephew, Toby, was one of the urchins. Very apt casting, I must say!' she added, her three chins wobbling in unison.

Jemma had glowed with pride. She was still slightly amazed by everything that had happened. The old dumpy Jemma Farrant, with her sludge-coloured hair and fat thighs, who never knew what to say to people and whose mother insisted on treating her like a ten-year-old was a thing of the past. Not only had she lost all that puppy fat, she was on her way to stardom. After her performance as Mandy Fincham's stand-in in the school play, everyone had showered her with congratulations.

Even her love life was looking good. She'd had a great time with Rob on New Year's Eve and he'd asked her to go out with him again. He'd even told her she was lovely. To think that Chelsea Gee, who had looks to die for and never felt nervous or unsure of anything, had really fancied him something rotten, but he'd chosen Jemma as a girlfriend! Perhaps it really was true – perhaps she did have star quality.

She could see it now in big bold type in the *Sky Guide*. *Jemma Farrant, the new star in theatre's firmament, comes to your screen as . . .* Now, what would it be? Juliet? Ophelia? Or perhaps Emma? They were doing Jane Austen for GCSE and she quite fancied swanning around in an empire-line dress fluttering a fan.

Jemma rammed her set books into her school bag. Of course, once GCSEs were over she would leave and go to drama school. She was going to be so busy this year. Miss Olive wanted her to do loads of different classes. She'd have to get her mum and dad to fork out for the rest. Gran had been really cool and given her the drama lessons for Christmas.

She turned her profile to the mirror, lifted her chin and surveyed her reflection. Now that she had lost weight, she really didn't look too bad. Of course, she'd have to get a perm, and highlights too probably, and maybe her eyelashes dyed . . . She'd have to ask Laura where she got hers done.

'Petal? You up there, poppet?' Her mother's voice tinkled up the stairs. Jemma cringed. The first thing she would have to do would be to sort her mother out once and for all. She'd have to realise that Jemma was on her way to fame and give her some respect – after all, she had even outshone Sumitha in the school musical and Sumitha had been singing and dancing for years. Jemma reckoned that was why Sumitha hadn't turned up at the party after the play; she couldn't handle the competition.

Still, she thought, scooping her hair up and wondering how she would look in period costume, she should be nice to her – it was understandable that she felt a bit overshadowed. Besides, she'd want someone to go to class with.

But Sumitha had other ideas.

Chapter Four

Sumitha Makes a Deal

'For the last time, will you get the hell out of my bed-room!' yelled Sumitha, hurling her history text book at her brother who was standing in the doorway, rubbing his left foot up and down his right leg and looking utterly pathetic.

'But I want you to . . .' he whined.

'You are such an utter and total wimp!' shouted his sister. 'For the last time, I have no intention of spending the rest of term walking to school with a Year Seven idiot and that is final!'

Sumitha knew that, if she timed it right, she could bump into Jon on his way to the Bellborough Court school coach. She certainly did not intend to have an eleven-year-old kid tagging along behind.

'Why can't you walk with your own friends?' she demanded.

'I want to go with you,' said Sandeep, his dark eyes fill-ing with tears, 'I don't like walking with them.'

'Oh, honestly, grow up, can't you?' snapped Sumitha. 'Don't be such a baby!'

She couldn't be doing with Sandeep trailing after her. He was turning into one pathetic kid. When he had started at Lee Hill the term before, he had really enjoyed it – then suddenly, after half-term, he had regressed to babyhood and started acting all pathetic, waiting for her at the end of the afternoon and insisting on sitting near her on the bus or sticking at her side like glue when they walked home. After the awful business with Bilu she had been pleased to have her brother as an excuse not to get involved in too many discussions with her friends, but she was over that now, and he was just being a pain. All last week he had shadowed her like a homesick puppy. Well, it was time she put her foot down. She was going to make a lot of changes in her life – and she wanted to talk to Jon.

Of course, after that terrible experience at the party, when she'd got drunk and thought she was going to die, she had vowed that she would never get involved with a boy again. Then Jon had invited her to The Stomping Ground for New Year's Eve. Half of her had wanted to go, because she really liked Jon as a mate, but the other half was scared that people would start talking about the mess-up with Bilu and make fun of her. So she had refused, saying she ought to stay at home with her family.

'OK, then,' Jon had said, 'suppose I come over to your house? That way your mum and dad wouldn't be upset about your going out.'

'You mean, you'd give up The Stomping Ground just to come over and listen to my father's boring sitar music droning on?' Sumitha had asked in amazement.

'If it meant being with you, of course I would,' Jon had said, turning beetroot and paying a great deal of attention to the floorboards.

So she had gone. And it had been OK. The best thing was that she could really talk to Jon. Not just idle chit-chat but really meaningful stuff. And there were no embarrassing overtones – Jon was just a mate. Nothing more.

He had told her all about how he wanted to be a cartoonist on a national newspaper. 'I want to be a political cartoonist – a sort of satirist with a pencil,' he'd said. (Sumitha had had to look up 'satirist' in the Oxford English Dictionary when she got home.) He'd explained that important issues like ethnic cleansing or famine in Africa needed to be highlighted and some people might find it easier to understand from looking at cartoons than reading political speeches. 'I want to do a job that makes me feel – oh, I don't know – as if I'm making a contribution and drawing is about the only thing I can imagine doing for the rest of my life,' he'd said. 'Does that sound rubbish?' he'd added, watching her anxiously.

'Of course it doesn't,' Sumitha had assured him, 'I think it's brilliant.'

Ever since then, Sumitha had done a lot of thinking. She realised just how clued up about the world Jon was and how certain about what he wanted to do with his life. Everything he did was geared to achieving his ambition. Bellborough Court, being a private school, didn't go back till a week after Lee Hill and Jon had even organised a work experience slot with the local newspaper. His single-minded determination suddenly made her own life seem so trivial and shallow, and now she wanted to sound him out on her new ideas. And she couldn't do that with her brother hanging around.

'Sandeep,' she called.

He peered round his bedroom door.

'Here's a pound – you can get yourself some sweets on the way to school as long as you let me walk on my own.'

Sandeep grabbed the one pound coin and stared at it with a look of relief on his face.

'Thanks,' he breathed. 'Thanks ever so much.'

Cheap at the price, thought Sumitha, surprised at having struck a deal so easily. She didn't stop to wonder why Sandeep was looking at that coin as though it was a lifeline.

Chapter Five

Laura Goes Green

'I do honestly think that Laura is calming down,' said Ruth to Melvyn on Monday morning, as sounds of a slightly off-key rendition of 'Love You to Pieces' floated up the stairs. 'I mean, she's actually got up and gone downstairs without us having to nag her every three minutes.'

'And by the sound of all that clattering, she's getting

breakfast ready too,' said Melvyn. 'Wonders will never cease.'

'She even seems to have accepted the baby coming,' added Ruth, surveying her expanding reflection with exasperation. 'Honestly, I'm fed up with wearing tracksuit trousers and baggy shirts but nothing else fits.'

'Well,' said Melvyn, kissing the back of her neck, 'when Tarquin arrives I'll buy you a whole new wardrobe.'

'You mean, when Phoebe is born!' joked Ruth.

'Whoever,' said Melvyn, smiling. 'Now, shall we go and see what culinary delight your daughter has created for breakfast?'

Unfortunately their good mood was broken when they walked into the kitchen.

'You two simply don't care, do you?' shouted Laura as they entered the kitchen. 'Daniel says that the survival of this planet is under threat just because of people like you.' She hurled the top off the pedal bin and rummaged through its rather odorous contents.

I think we spoke too soon, thought Ruth, looking around in vain for signs of breakfast.

'Now what have we done?' asked Melvyn.

'It's what you haven't done,' retorted Laura. 'All these apple peelings should be put on to the compost heap and . . .'

'We don't have a compost heap,' pointed out Melvyn reasonably, putting some bacon rashers under the grill.

'Well, we should have!' declared Laura. 'Daniel says

19

that your generation are simply not fit custodians of our future.'

'Who's Daniel?' asked Melvyn.

'The lad next door,' Ruth reminded him. 'You know, the Brownings' son. We met him on New Year's Eve.'

'Oh, him,' said Melvyn. 'Intense guy, floppy hair. Laura, it's twenty to eight. Shouldn't you be leaving for school?'

'And look at this!' shouted Laura, ignoring him and fishing a Coca Cola can from the debris.

'Laura, what are you going on about?' asked her mother wearily. Her back was aching, her unborn child was practising rugby tackles against her ribcage and glad as she was that Laura had made friends with the boy next door, she was not in the mood to have his opinions foisted on her. 'Three weeks ago, you hadn't even met Daniel – now it seems he is the world expert on everything.'

Laura gave her a withering look. 'That's right, libel my friends . . .'

'Slander,' corrected Melvyn, slapping bread into the toaster.

'Pardon?' said Laura.

'Slander,' repeated Melvyn. 'Slander is spoken, libel is written.'

'Oh very clever. You should be taking all this stuff to the recycling centre.'

Ruth sighed. 'Laura, I put the newspapers out for

collection, I take our bottles to the bottle bank, I send our old clothes to the Salvation Army – what more do you want me to do? I don't have time to sort through every last egg shell. And at six and a half months' pregnant, I don't want to be humping boxes halfway round the countryside.'

'That's another thing. You are adding to an already over-populated world. Daniel says . . .'

'Oh, for Pete's sake!' snapped Ruth, as the baby decided to try out a bit of goal shooting practice on her bladder. 'I don't give two hoots what Daniel says. If he's so bothered about my unrecycled margarine tubs, let him come and sort them out. And if we are talking about putting rubbish to good use, why not start in your bedroom? There's enough junk and debris in there to keep even the most ardent conservationist happy for hours.'

Laura glowered and grabbed a blueberry yoghurt.

'That's not enough for you to go to school on,' said Melvyn. 'Want a bacon sandwich?'

'Come off it, you know I'm a vegetarian now,' said Laura glaring at him.

'All the same, there's nothing to beat a good bacon sarnie early in the morning,' said Melvyn.

'Don't you care about those poor little pigs?' shouted Laura, pocketing a banana and two apples from the fruit bowl. 'If I told you what they do to pigs . . .'

'Go to school,' said her mother.

'I shall,' said Laura, and stormed out.

Chapter Six

Chelsea Gets the Monday Morning Blues

'Chelsea! It's half past seven!' Her mother knocked on her door and marched in.

'Oh, for heaven's sake, Chelsea,' she exclaimed, 'this room is a tip. I asked you specifically to clear it up yesterday – you haven't touched it!'

'So?' mumbled Chelsea, crawling out from under the duvet. 'It's my room – what's it got to do with you, anyway?'

'I beg your pardon, young lady?' said her mother, yanking back the curtains. 'It has everything to do with me. I've got a long day ahead – editorial meeting, radio show this afternoon . . .'

'So? That's your problem,' said Chelsea.

Ginny grabbed her daughter by the arm. 'Now, just you listen here. I will not be spoken to like that by you or anybody else, and while you live—'

'While you live under my roof, you live by my rules,' chanted Chelsea sarcastically, shrugging off her mother's grasp. 'Change the track, won't you?'

She grabbed her dressing gown, pushed past her mother and thundered into the bathroom.

Ginny sighed and sank down on the end of Chelsea's bed. Here we go again, she thought. Ever since the end of last term, Chelsea had been as prickly as a hedgehog. What was happening to her? Come to that, what was happening to all of them? Just lately, all the fun seemed to have gone out of life. Barry had insisted on working on Boxing Day and at New Year, and when he wasn't working he was moaning at her for spending too much money, or shutting himself in the kitchen to practise his recipes for the final of *Superchef*. Please God, let him win – they could do with the ten thousand pound prize money and, besides, it would cheer Barry up. A bit of cheering up was in order all round. She had taken on this new radio show to boost their income, but she felt so tired all the time, and bloated and fat – and, well, old. It just wasn't like her; she'd always been so full of bounce. She had even been to see the doctor and he had told her it was her age, at which point she felt like throwing his stethoscope at him and storming out. But then he had offered her this new HRT treatment which he assured her would work wonders. She wished it would hurry up.

She knew her writing was losing its usual sparkle too – twice last month the editor had made comments like, 'Write like you used to in the old days,' and, 'Let's have some more of the Jesting Ginny.' I'll give him Jesting Ginny, she thought darkly. What does he know – thirty-two, double income, no kids. He doesn't know he's born.

She surveyed the rubbish heap that Chelsea laughingly called a bedroom. She gave a half-hearted yank to the duvet, revealed two sordid apple cores and a dented Pepsi can, and decided against it.

'Coffee!' she told herself sternly. She knew she should be drinking camomile tea or infusion of rose petal or some such healthy beverage but this morning she needed caffeine. Ginny was a great believer in caffeine as a cure for nearly every ill.

'What was all that about?' said Barry, looking up from his new copy of *Top Taste* magazine as Ginny came into the kitchen and wondering, not for the first time, whether lime green and mango was really the best colour combination for his wife's outfit.

'Oh, the usual – Chelsea hasn't cleaned her room, and – oh, forget it.'

'Still sulking about not having a party, is she?' asked Barry. 'A meal at Lorenzo's and that's it. I'll book a table for Saturday. Set menu, mind you. Now that I'm renting that catering unit over on the industrial estate, we've got to keep an even tighter rein.'

'Great,' muttered Ginny, blotting her lipstick.

'You were the one who wanted me out of the kitchen,' said Barry.

Ginny sighed. 'I know, I know, and I suppose we must make allowances for Chelsea,' she said. 'After all, she's a teenager who has split with the guy she fancied and now we're saying that she can't have a party; it's natural that she should be volatile. We must just keep calm and let it flow over us.'

Chelsea hurtled into the kitchen and headed for the bread bin.

'CHELSEA!' shrieked Ginny, all thoughts of serenity forgotten. 'What have you got on?'

'Clothes, surprisingly,' said Chelsea, smearing Flora on to her bread with one hand and giving an ineffectual tug to her black miniskirt with the other.

'By the way,' said Ginny brightly, trying to calm down and change the subject, 'Dad said you were with a crowd of kids he didn't recognise when he picked you up at New Year – new friends, are they?'

'They might be,' said Chelsea non-committally. She did rather like Bex, but Fee terrified her and Trug was a bit weird.

'You could invite one of them out for your birthday meal, if you like,' her father said, picking up the signs from Ginny.

For an instant, Chelsea almost smiled.

'Mind you, you can give the loudmouthed weird one a miss – and the rest would have to smarten up for Lorenzo's,' Barry added.

Ginny raised an eyebrow at him. Too late.

'Oh, that's right, go on, trash my friends, why don't you?' shouted Chelsea. 'That's typical of your generation – judge a person by their looks. Well, if we all did that, you'd be certified a right loony.'

And with that she grabbed her school bag, hurled the remainder of her sandwich into the bin and stormed out through the back door.

'Well done, dear,' said Ginny.

'I never seem to get it right,' said Barry dolefully.

'You and me both,' said his wife consolingly. 'Have another cup of coffee.'

Chelsea stood at the bus stop, distancing herself from the crowd of Year Sevens who were giggling over a boyband poster, and idly kicking a stone with her toe. She hated herself. She hated life. Why was she so crabby all the time? It wasn't even as if it was that time of the month. She just felt all cold and black and miserable inside, as if she didn't know who she was any more. Everything was changing. Geneva and Warwick had left home so she had no one to take her side any more. Even her body was turning against her. She was getting spots, which she had never had before, and she felt moody and miserable and restless and utterly fed up.

She had thought she would feel better once term started, but how could she feel good when every break time she had to witness Jemma and Rob mooning all over one another, not to mention suffer the humiliation of her father's van parked outside the gates selling his crummy soup?

And now all she had to look forward to was a meal at Lorenzo's when what she really wanted was to chill out with a party for all her mates from school. She'd ask Laura to come with her – that would appease her. And Sumitha too. They would jump at the chance. She was, after all, still their best friend.

Chapter Seven

Jemma Turns a Drama into a Crisis

'Oh, I get it!' shouted Jemma, slamming the drama school prospectus down on the kitchen counter top and wheeling round to face her mother.

'You just can't bear to see me succeed, can you? You can't cope with the fact that I've got talent, that I'm going to achieve more in life than spending my days cutting out sticky paper shapes and making elephants out of egg boxes for some stupid crèche. You're jealous!'

'Oh, petal, don't be so silly,' began her mother, who in between pouring Frosties into bowls for the twins and per-suading Sam not to be a dinosaur under the breakfast table, was sticking copious quantities of cotton wool on to a loo roll in an attempt to create a snowman for the crèche's Winter Wonderland display. 'I just—'

'How many more times do I have to tell you – don't call me petal!' snarled Jemma. 'I'm not a kid any more, even though I know you'd like to have me on leading reins with a bib round my neck even now!'

'Have you quite finished?' asked her mum, dragging Sam from under the table and plonking him on a chair. 'All I said was that you simply cannot go to drama class *and* mime *and* elocution. Gran gave you the cash for one year's course. You have to make a choice. And hurry up with that egg – it's nearly ten to eight.'

'I'll eat it,' offered Sam, hopefully.

'But Miss Olive said I had wonderful stage presence and that I needed to do all three to maximise my star potential!' protested Jemma, flicking her hair out of her eyes and shoving her boiled egg at her brother.

'Maximise her takings, more like!' muttered Mrs Farrant, sticking a cardboard top hat on to her snowman and standing back to admire her handiwork.

Jemma pushed back her chair and jumped to her feet. 'At last I've discovered who I am and where I'm going. I'm going to be a star – and you're not going to stop me.'

'Look, Jemma—' her mother began, but Jemma had snatched up the prospectus and flounced out of the kitchen. Two minutes later the front door slammed.

'What's Jemma doin', Mum?' asked Luke, sticking his finger into Sam's egg.

'Being fourteen,' muttered Claire, closing her eyes and counting to ten. Her friends had warned her about the teenage years; whenever she had said that little Jemma was no trouble they had winked at each other and said, 'She'll learn soon enough,' but she had never expected her compliant daughter to turn all moody and argumentative – and so suddenly. She did hope this drama idea wasn't going to spoil little Jemma. Claire's mother had been so thrilled by her granddaughter's performance as Nancy in the school

28

production of *Oliver!* that she had said she wanted to foster her talent.

'It'll be something all of her own to do – give her some independence,' she had said meaningfully when Claire took her to the airport to see her off on her long-awaited trip to China. Independence was all very well, thought Claire, but she didn't want Jemma turning into one of those difficult teenagers. Some of those drama student types looked so odd and she didn't want Jemma exposed to unsavoury elements. Still, it was probably just a phase. It wouldn't last.

Chapter Eight

Jon and Sumitha Get Their Wires Crossed

When Jon rounded the corner of Billing Hill and saw Sumitha walking along Wellington Road, he could hardly believe his luck. Ever since New Year's Eve he had been thinking about her and wanting to ask her out again but he'd been a bit wary of phoning her in case her dad answered. Rajiv Banerji was not desperately keen on his daughter having boyfriends and having got Sumitha interested, he was not about to do anything that might wreck things.

Actually, he admitted to himself, he wasn't even sure

that Sumitha saw him as boyfriend material. She'd been really chatty at the club, but every time Jon had tried to kiss her, or get close, she'd pulled away. She'd seemed more keen to talk than anything else. Probably the fault of that slime bag, Bilu, he thought to himself. He'd just have to win her round slowly.

Sumitha saw him from across the road and beckoned. Why, this morning of all mornings, did he have to have pimples the size of Smarties on his chin? He pulled his scarf over his face and hoped they didn't show.

'Hi!' said Sumitha as Jon joined her. 'I'm glad I've seen you – I need to talk to you about something.'

Jon grinned at her. 'You look terrific,' he said, wondering if he dared kiss her.

'Do I? Thanks,' said Sumitha. 'The thing is . . . well . . .' She hesitated.

'Yes?' prompted Jon, heading for the bus stop.

'No, stay here a minute,' she pleaded. 'I don't want your mates to hear.'

Jon stopped obediently in his tracks and gazed at her. She had such cute ear lobes, he thought. He wanted to nibble them.

'Well, being with you on New Year's Eve – it just made me see my whole life differently,' she said. 'I've never felt like it before.'

Oh, wow! thought Jon. This is it. She's fallen in love with me. Yes! Score! WOWEEE!

Visions of him and Sumitha kissing in the moonlight,

him and Sumitha walking hand in hand through town, all his mates green with envy at his gorgeous girlfriend, floated before his eyes.

'. . . and you made me see I can't afford to waste any more time,' Sumitha was saying.

Jon smiled dreamily. She loved him. She knew that denying her feelings was a waste of time. She was declaring her love. He felt ten feet tall. He could actually feel his spots shrinking.

'. . . you're right, we simply have to do something . . .' she said.

'Yes,' breathed Jon, taking her hand.

He couldn't believe his luck.

'And we can't go on putting off decisions for ever,' she continued, removing her hand.

'That's right,' agreed Jon. She knew she had to make a commitment to him. She was in love with him, Jon Joseph. Jon and Sumitha. Sumitha and Jon. His heart kept lurching in a most undisciplined manner.

'But I can't make up my mind what I ought to do,' said Sumitha. 'I mean, I can't keep on with all these dancing classes and drama and stuff, if I'm going to . . .'

'Oh, I don't mind if you do,' said Jon magnanimously, gazing at her adoringly and taking her hand once more. 'There'll still be plenty of time for us.'

Sumitha snatched it away again.

'Have you been listening to a word I've been saying?' she snapped.

'Of course I have,' said Jon hastily. 'You think you should give up dancing now we're an item and—'

'IN YOUR DREAMS!' shouted Sumitha. 'Where are you at? And to think that I thought that with you I could have a rational, meaningful conversation. You're as bad as all the rest.'

She snatched up her school bag and flounced off.

'No, wait – no, Sumitha please!' Jon started after her, trying to ignore the titters from the other guys waiting for the bus. 'Sumitha – stop.'

She was just turning reluctantly to face him when a voice said, 'Hello, son!' and to his horror his father, clad in a purple and white tracksuit, and with a white towel draped round his neck, jogged round the corner. Ever since Jon had introduced him to the gym, his father had gone totally over the top on the fitness front and was now jogging every morning before work. His face was puce and little rivulets of sweat were dribbling down his pudgy cheeks. Three hairs of uneven length protruded from his left nostril. He was not an attractive sight.

'Four miles and counting,' he boomed, hammering his chest like a demented King Kong. 'Oh, and this must be – now, let me think – Semelda, isn't it?'

'Sumitha,' said Sumitha. 'Hi, Mr Joseph.'

'Of course, of course,' said Henry, running on the spot and panting like a bulldog with sunstroke. 'So you're the new girlfriend m'boy's so mad over, are you? Well, so his mother tells me.'

'Dad!' hissed Jon. How could he? How could he? How totally embarrassing!

'Well, jolly good, fine by me, all in favour of young love. Haha! – and no need to worry, Semelda, dear – no racial prejudice in our house. Won't find me criticising you Bengalis, not like some I could mention. Broad-minded as the next man, I am. Must keep moving – two miles to go! Bye, Jon, bye Semelda!'

And he pounded off, waving airily as he went. Jon hoped the pavement would open up and swallow him whole.

'I'm sorry, my dad's so—' began Jon.

'That's your bus,' muttered Sumitha through pursed lips as the Bellborough Court coach pulled up.

'I'll phone you tonight!' called Jon. After I've finished murdering my father and pickling him in formaldehyde, he thought bitterly.

'Don't bother!' shouted Sumitha. 'You won't listen to a word I say anyway. And just for the record, how dare you go around telling people I'm your girlfriend? How dare you!'

Jon looked forlornly out of the bus window as Sumitha hurried up the road. Trust me to blow it, he thought. Why did his mum have to go spouting out about Sumitha to his dad? I'll never tell her anything ever again, he thought. Parents! 'Talk to us,' they say and then, when you do, they broadcast it to the whole world. He wished his mother was more like she used to be. Ever since she had started at the art college, she had gone all matey and giggly and started wearing jeans that were too tight for her and acting like someone half her age, pretending she understood what made Jon tick, when in fact she hadn't a clue. His dad said she was making up for lost time. Jon wished she'd do it somewhere else.

Not that his dad was any less of a liability, Jon thought. How could he say those things? I'll kill him.

It was then it occurred to him that he never did discover what Sumitha was actually trying to tell him.

Chapter Nine

Jemma Fails to Take Centre Stage

'Hi, Sumitha — guess what?' Jemma rammed her books into her locker and turned eagerly to face Sumitha.

'What?' said Sumitha shortly. She was still seething over Jon's lack of attention to her dilemma. She had so wanted to tell him about her idea of becoming a foreign correspondent and, what with his total lack of concentration on what she was saying and Mr Joseph's patronising and racist attitude, she was certainly not in the mood to be enthusiastic about anything.

'I'm doing drama at the same place as you — I went to

see Miss Olive last Saturday,' Jemma announced triumphantly. 'We can go together.'

'No, we can't,' said Sumitha, fishing in her pocket for a comb.

'Why not? You go on Thursdays and Saturdays, don't you?' asked Jemma.

'I went on Thursdays and Saturdays,' corrected Sumitha. 'I'm giving it up.'

'You're what?' Jemma was incredulous. 'What on earth for?'

Sumitha was about to explain when Laura crashed into the cloakroom, clutching a pile of rubbish to her chest.

'Hi, you guys,' she panted. 'Has anyone got a carrier bag?'

'Yes, somewhere I think,' said Sumitha, scrabbling in her locker. 'Here you are – it's a bit tatty, I'm afraid.'

'Doesn't matter,' said Laura and tipped a collection of bent Coke cans, crumpled sweet wrappers and old comics into the bag.

'What on earth . . . ?' began Sumitha.

'This lot was in the bins by the art block,' said Laura. 'It's disgusting!'

'You're telling me!' said Sumitha, wrinkling her nose. 'But if it was in the bin, why take it all out again?'

'Because,' said Laura emphatically, 'all this shouldn't be chucked away – it should be recycled. Did you know,' she continued, staring at them sternly, 'that every adult in this country throws out ten times their own body weight in rubbish every year?'

'Fancy,' said Jemma. 'Anyway, Sumitha, as I was saying. Miss Olive said that I had great potential—'

'Laura, is that really true? Ten times your body weight? That's incredible,' said Sumitha. 'So what are you going to do?'

'Well, I'm going to ask Mr Horage if I can set up a recycling scheme at school,' said Laura. 'I mean, I know we have newspaper collections and stuff but if we had bins for cans, bins for bottles, bins for plastic . . .'

'You couldn't fit in a bin for infuriating males, could you?' said Sumitha.

'Why? What's up?' asked Laura. Surely Sumitha and Jon couldn't have had a falling out. Could they? Possibly?

'Well,' began Sumitha, and she and Laura drifted in the direction of the classroom.

'Wait for me!' called Jemma. 'I was just saying about . . .'
But Sumitha and Laura had gone.

I suppose, thought Jemma to herself, rearranging her hair in the mirror, that Sumitha just can't cope with being outshone. That's why she changed the subject. Come to think of it, that's probably why she's dropping the whole thing. You can't help feeling sorry for her. She's met her match.

Chapter Ten

Consolation Over Coffee

'Features desk – Ginny Gee speaking.'

'Hi, Ginny? It's me, Ruth.' Laura's mum rearranged her bottom on the kitchen stool and tucked the telephone under her chin.

'Yes?'

'Oh, er – sorry. Have I caught you at a bad time?' asked Ruth, sensing the abrupt tone to Ginny's voice.

'Every time is bad these days,' muttered Ginny, who was endeavouring to write a feature on ten ways to revitalise a marriage and was only on way number one.

'Don't worry – I'll call you later,' said Ruth, shifting her position as the baby's head butted her navel.

'No – no, hang on, Roo – I'm sorry. It's just that . . . oh, well never mind. What can I do for you?'

'Well, I've got to come into town for an ante-natal appointment and I was just wondering whether we could meet for a bite of lunch. But don't worry, we can make it another day.'

'I might not make it through another day,' said Ginny, sounding perilously close to tears. 'No, lunch would be great – just what I need. Meet you outside Lawrence's at, say, twelve-thirty?'

Ruth surveyed her friend anxiously. They had grabbed a

corner table and were ensconced with their tuna mayonnaise baguettes and a large pot of coffee.

'What's up?' she asked her directly. It was obvious something was wrong; the normally garrulous Ginny was absently stirring her coffee and looking thoroughly fed up.

'Oh,' sighed Ginny. 'I don't know. I just feel so disillusioned – tired of churning out flippant little features which in all probability no one ever reads.' She nibbled at a hangnail and sighed again.

'Of course they read them!' exclaimed Ruth. 'Your articles are a tonic – they always make me laugh. And you've got this new radio slot – what's it called?'

'*Live Lines to Ginny,*' said Ginny. 'People phone in with their problems and I supposedly chat to them on air and make them feel better.' She turned to face Ruth. 'But I ask you – who am I to help anyone? I can't even sort my own life out. Take today – writing about revitalising your marriage. Me – whose marriage is about as vitalised as a collapsed soufflé.'

Ruth giggled. 'There you are, you see – you're funny even when you're miserable. But surely, things are looking up, aren't they?' she asked anxiously when Ginny didn't smile. 'Barry's business seems to be going strong – I'm always seeing the van parked in some lay-by or other. And you, well, you're everywhere – newspaper, radio, magazines. Perhaps you should go to the doctor?' she added, concerned.

'I did,' said Ginny. 'About two weeks ago. He said what

he always says: it's the menopause. Well I knew that. I'm no stranger to wayward hormones and proliferating flesh.' She pulled a face. 'He's put me on HRT.'

'There you are then!' exclaimed Ruth. 'You'll feel a million dollars in no time. But you have to persevere, Ginny. I read that too many women give up before giving it a chance – you have to wait a month or two.'

'I suppose so,' sighed Ginny. 'Anyway, enough of me – how is this infant behaving itself?' She gestured at Ruth's stomach with a grin. 'What did they say at the clinic?'

'Apart from the fact that it never manages to stay still for more than ten minutes at a time, everything is fine,' said Ruth. 'Sometimes I think I'll be glad when March the twelfth comes and I can see my feet again, but at least while it's still in there, it can't accuse me of single-handedly causing the demise of our planet.'

'Pardon?' said Ginny.

'Laura,' said Ruth. 'Into ecology in a big way this week.'

Ginny sighed. 'Well, at least she's into something,' she said. 'These days Chelsea seems to be making a profes- sional study of lolling about.'

'Well, thank goodness the kids are back at school,' said Ruth comfortingly. 'That gives us ten weeks' comparative respite!'

It was a remark she was to remember in the weeks to come.

Chapter Eleven

A Scientific Miracle

'Hey, guess what, old Mellor's not coming back this term!' announced Laura to the others as their science set waited for class to start.

'Really? You mean we've seen the last of Smelly Melly?' asked Sumitha.

'Awesome!' gasped Chelsea.

Miss Mellor, who despite being a science graduate of some note had never quite grasped the purpose of either depilatory creams or anti-perspirant, was not one of Lee Hill's most cherished teachers.

'Mr Horage told me,' said Laura. 'Let's hope we get someone halfway decent,' she added. 'It's bad enough having to do photosynthesis and heat conduction and all that boring stuff without having an prehistoric reptile teaching us. Sumitha?'

Sumitha was staring open-mouthed over Laura's left shoulder. Laura turned just as a gorgeous guy in denim jeans and what had to be a Ralph Lauren Polo shirt strode into the room and perched on the edge of the desk.

'Good morning, everyone,' he said brightly, running his fingers through thick black hair. 'I'm Paul Sharpe and I'm your new science teacher.'

A murmur of approval ran through the room, and a

number of the girls began fiddling with their fringes and straightening their skirts.

Not bad, thought Laura.

This is better, thought Chelsea.

He is without exception the most gorgeous guy I have ever seen, thought Sumitha.

'What happened to Smelly Mel – Miss Mellor, sir?' asked Chelsea with a grin.

Mr Sharpe didn't blink an eyelid. 'She has gone to do some research at an institute in Washington for a year,' he said.

'It'll be whiffy in Washington,' chirped a bright spark.

'Now, let me tell you a bit about myself,' said Mr Sharpe, ignoring the jibe. 'I expect you are wondering what you have been landed with!' he added with a grin.

A hunk, thought Sumitha. A glorious, divine hunk.

'I have just come back to the UK after a year helping with a health and education project in India,' he said. 'And to help us get to know one another a bit better, I thought we might spend this first period looking at a video that gives you some idea of what scientists and engineers and researchers are doing to give positive help to underprivileged sections of the Indian community.' He turned and smiled. Straight at me, I know it, thought Sumitha – and as his charcoal eyes crinkled and his nose bunched into dear little creases, Sumitha knew. She was going to do what he had done. Whatever that was. Sumitha was going to be the best scientist Lee Hill had ever produced. For him. For Mr Sharpe. Paul.

41

Chapter Twelve

Sumitha Restructures Her Life

On Monday evening, Sumitha walked home from school, reliving every second of the science lesson. Mr Sharpe – Paul, as she whispered to herself over and over again – had talked with such passion about the village in India where he had worked. She had leaned back in her chair and let the grave tones float over her as he described how the team built a small laboratory for the rural school, how he – Paul – had masterminded evening classes for children who had to work on the land, and how he would love to initiate a twinning scheme between Lee Hill and Phorabadur. And at the end, as everyone was filing out of the room, she had lingered, taking as long as possible to pack her books into her bag and then it had happened. He had walked over to her and said, 'May I ask what part of India your family come from?'

'Calcutta, sir,' she had said.

'A fascinating city,' Mr Sharpe had enthused. 'I stayed there for several weeks when I first arrived, before moving to Phorabadur. I loved it.'

Sumitha glowed with pleasure as if she had personally built Calcutta for his delectation and delight.

'I suppose you speak fluent Bengali?' he asked. 'Perhaps I can practise my scant knowledge on you sometime?'

Sumitha gulped. They rarely spoke anything but English at home – the only time she got to practise was when they went to visit her grandparents once every two years. She'd spent most of the time moaning that she was English and didn't want to speak anything else. She smiled enigmatically.

'Are you keen on science?' asked Mr Sharpe. 'It's all right,' he added, grinning broadly, 'you are allowed to say no.'

'Oh, yes, yes –I love it,' said Sumitha, who until that moment had viewed science as just another necessary evil to be got through in the school day. 'I want to be a scientist.'

'Great stuff!' said Mr Sharpe enthusiastically. 'We'll have to talk some more. But come on, you'll be late for your next lesson.'

'We'll have to talk some more; we'll have to talk some more,' Sumitha repeated mantra-like in her head. That must mean he likes me, she thought. It was his way of letting me know that he liked me. From now on, I'm going to work flat out and be top in science. Just for him. Just for Paul.

'Sumitha, Sumitha, wait for me!' Sandeep came running up behind her, panting hard.

'What do you want now?' asked Sumitha in decidedly unsisterly tones.

'Can I walk with you?' he looked up at her appealingly.

'Oh, Sandeep, do you have to?' exclaimed Sumitha.

'You never stop talking and I am trying to think. Anyway, I saw you just now with Kevin and Matthew – why don't you walk with them?'

'I don't like them,' he whispered.

'Oh, grow up,' said Sumitha.

'Well, can I have some more money, if I promise not to walk with you?' suggested Sandeep brightening a little.

'No way! That was a one-off so if you are looking for more, forget it!'

Sandeep's face fell. 'Please, Mifa,' he said, reverting to the name he had called her when he was a toddler. 'Please.'

'I said no. Oh, for goodness' sake, if you're going to be a jerk, just walk and don't speak, OK?'

So preoccupied was she with her own thoughts that Sumitha did not notice the look of sheer relief on her brother's face.

Chapter Thirteen

Sumitha Bows Out

'I'd like to give up ballet and drama,' announced Sumitha over the supper table. Her parents looked up in surprise.

'But why should you want to do that?' enquired her mother. 'You are so good at that sort of thing. Has something happened?'

'No, but what is the point?' said Sumitha. 'What good will it do the world at large? What good will it do my career?'

This is new, thought Chitrita, passing Sandeep a plate of food and muttering, 'Elbows, Sandeep,' automatically as she did so.

Her father laid down his knife and fork and eyed his daughter with interest. 'And what career did you have in mind, Sumitha?' he asked. 'I wasn't aware that you had any idea of what you wanted to do until you marry.'

'Oh, Dad,' shouted Sumitha. 'What are you on? Until I marry? Why should marrying – if I do, which I might not – make any difference? Get real!'

She has a point, thought Chitrita. Although it took me long enough to persuade Rajiv to let me teach. 'What would you like to do, Sumitha?' she asked. 'Sandeep, eat!'

'I am going,' said Sumitha, taking a deep breath, 'to be a scientist. I won't have time for all these out of school activities because I'm going to be doing loads of work and experiments and stuff and get good grades and go to university. I am going to – to change the world.'

Her father roared with laughter. 'Single-handed, my child is going to do what no one has done in two millennia,' he chortled. Sumitha glared at him.

'All right then, make a difference in the world,' she

amended. 'Go ahead, laugh at me. Why? Because I'm a girl? That's it, isn't it, Dad? If Sandeep said he wanted to do science, you'd be telling him what a great guy he was. Boys can do anything in your eyes, girls are for cooking and having babies. You are so behind the times.'

'But Sumitha,' interrupted her mother, 'I did not even know that you were keen on science. You have never shown any special interest in it and—'

'Well, I am now!' retaliated Sumitha. 'Mr Sharpe was saying—'

'Mr Sharpe?' queried Chitrita.

'He's our new science teacher,' said Sumitha. 'He's amazing.'

Ah ha, thought Chitrita.

'Well, Sumitha,' said her father, 'you are wrong if you think I am not pleased. It is most commendable that you are beginning to turn your attention to serious pursuits. But why should this interest mean you give up your leisure activities?'

'Because,' said Sumitha, preparing to present them with her coup de grâce, 'I want to improve my Bengali.'

Her father's eyes widened. 'Well, of course,' he said. 'I think that is an excellent idea. You will be able to converse with your grandparents and uncles when we visit Calcutta in the summer.'

'Does that mean you'll be walking home every evening?' asked Sandeep hopefully.

'Yes, but not with you,' snapped Sumitha.

Sandeep stared morosely into his dinner.

'Don't be horrid to your brother,' said her mother automatically. 'And Sumitha, why this sudden interest in Bengali?'

'Does there have to be a reason?' asked Sumitha. 'I thought you'd be pleased – Dad's always going on about our culture.'

'I am delighted, my dear,' said her father, patting her on the shoulder. 'This is good news indeed, is it not, Chitrita?'

Chitrita smiled and inclined her head. She decided to reserve judgement. She just wondered whether her daughter's sudden interest in matters scientific had a basis in something rather less academic. The thought was so worrying that she she failed to notice that Sandeep had not eaten one bite of his supper.

Chapter Fourteen

Jon Lets Rip

'I have never, ever been so embarrassed in my whole life!' stormed Jon, hurling his rugby kit on the floor and glaring at his mother. 'How could you do that to me?'

'Do what?' asked Anona, holding up a swatch of lilac silk to the light and eyeing it critically. Her current college assignment was to convert an old screen into 'an elegant accessory for the home' and she was having problems with it.

'Tell Dad that I fancied Sumitha,' snarled Jon.

'I said no such thing!' denied his mother, chucking the fabric on the table and picking up a tape measure. 'What are you talking about?'

'I was talking to Sumitha and Dad rolls up and says "Oh, so you're the one my boy fancies," or something like that! And then he said you had told him! How could you?'

'Oh, I remember,' said Anona, through a mouthful of pins. 'Dad asked me who the girl in the portrait in your room was, and I said – oh, well, I suppose I did say you had your eye on her.'

'Oh well, great. Marvellous. Thanks for nothing, Mum. Well, you will be pleased to know that between you, you've managed to ruin any chances I had of even being friends with Sumitha. I hope you're satisfied.'

'Look, I'm sure it's not as bad as . . .' began his mother. 'Where are you going?' she added, as Jon headed for the door.

'Out,' said Jon.

Chapter Fifteen

Laura Lays Plans

Tuesday was a very good day for Laura. For one thing, Mr Horage announced that they would try out her recycling idea for one term to see if it worked.

'We can't do everything at once,' he said, 'but we'll try it out with aluminium cans and paper because that's the sort of stuff you kids have most of at school.'

'But sir,' said Laura, 'what about glass and plastics? And we should stop the cafeteria selling meat products, and then perhaps we should—'

'Hang on a minute, Laura,' said Mr Horage, laughing. 'This is a school, not a centre for ecological enlightenment. I admire your principles but we must start slowly. We will put recycling bins in the yard by the science block and some more outside the gym. You can use the notice-board in the top corridor to publicise what you are doing – with your flair for words you should be able to catch people's attention.'

Laura felt mollified. She would abandon the novel for the time being and devote herself to promoting ecological awareness.

'You'll help, won't you, Chelsea?' she asked.

'I suppose so,' sighed Chelsea.

'Don't let your enthusiasm run away with you,' said Laura sarcastically.

That evening, while she was writing posters for the noticeboard, Daniel phoned to check that she was going to the demo on Saturday morning.

'Wear something really warm,' he instructed, 'because we sit down and don't move a lot. Oh, and can you make a poster or a placard or something?'

'OK,' said Laura. Daniel had, she thought, potential. She wanted to have a boyfriend and, even though Sumitha was in a mood with Jon at the moment, she knew Jon had eyes for no one else.

She was ten minutes into making her placard when her father phoned. She hadn't seen him since before Christmas because the Bestial Betsy had insisted that they should take soppy Sonia and drippy Daryl to stay with their grandmother in Norfolk for the holiday. What's more, she was still waiting for her Christmas present from him.

'Hi, sweetie,' he said. 'Look, how about I take you out for a meal on Saturday evening? Just you and me,' he emphasised, knowing Laura's antipathy towards Betsy. 'We could make it a belated Christmas celebration – and there's something I want to talk to you about.'

And something you want to give me, I hope, thought Laura.

'Great, Dad,' she said. 'By the way, do you recycle?'

'No, love, I always take the car.'

'I said recycle, not cycle,' said Laura.

'Oh, that,' said Peter. There was a long pause.

'Dad? Are you there?'

'Yes, sweetie, just having a sip of my Scotch. No, recycling and all that stuff – that's Betsy's department – she'd re-use a teabag given half a chance. Do you know, she even saves those slivers of soap that get left at the end of a bar and sticks them all together to make another one? Crazy or what?'

It was a pity, thought Laura, that Betsy was a homebreaker and a man-snatcher. Otherwise she could have quite admired her.

'That's a good idea,' said Laura. 'Daniel says . . .'

There was another gulping noise. 'Who's Daniel?' asked her father.

'I'll explain on Saturday,' said Laura. 'Dad, are you OK?'

'Me? Oh, yes, fine. But I'll be all the better for seeing you.'

'See you on Saturday then,' said Laura. Her father really did sound rather weird.

Chapter Sixteen

Help! I Need Somebody

Any hopes that Chelsea had about things getting better had faded by Wednesday. On Monday, Miss McConnell had a go at her for not completing her French assignment and told her that life did not owe her a living and that she was wasting a good brain and should start pulling her weight.

On Tuesday during lunch hour, she asked Laura if she would go out to Lorenzo's for her birthday meal.

'Oh, sorry – I can't – I'm going out with my dad,' said Laura.

'Well, OK, how about we go shopping in the morning instead?' Chelsea suggested. 'You can help me spend the birthday money I hope I am going to get.'

'Can't,' said Laura. 'I'm going to a demo with Daniel.'

'A what?' queried Chelsea.

'A demonstration outside Leehampton Labs,' explained Laura. 'They do all this cruel testing on rabbits and cats and stuff. Why don't you come?'

'No thanks,' said Chelsea. 'Anyway, what's the point? They've got to test the stuff somehow and they can't do it on people so they do it on animals.'

'That's a terrible attitude!' shouted Laura. 'How can you be so complacent! It would be better not to have make-up at all than to make animals suffer for our vanity!'

Chelsea shrugged. 'Anyway, it's my birthday – can't you do your righteous bit another week?' she grumbled.

'Oh, so Chelsea Gee's birthday is more important than an animal's life, is it? Well, great. And I thought you were my friend!'

And she flounced off to geography. Chelsea was stunned. Of course she was Laura's friend. They had been friends for years. It was an accepted fact. Come to think of it, talking of friendship, how could Laura let her down like that? Surely her birthday was more important that some stupid protest?

Sumitha will come, thought Chelsea on Tuesday evening and rang her number. But Sumitha declined her offer since her father was taking her to the radiology unit with him so she could observe one of his shifts.

'Oh, very exciting!' said Chelsea cuttingly. 'Can't you do that some other time?'

'Not really,' said Sumitha.

'Great,' said Chelsea.

What made it worse was that on Wednesday, her father said, 'I've booked the table for four – who are you bringing?'

'Not sure yet,' Chelsea mumbled. 'I'll tell you tomorrow.'

It was so humiliating. Every other fifteen-year-old had a boyfriend to take; but every boy she fancied disappeared. Rob, Guy . . . She had a flash of inspiration.

'Porter's Lodge, how may I help you?'

'I'd like to speak to Guy Griffiths please, but I don't know what hall of residence he's in.' Chelsea's heart was pounding.

'Wait a moment, miss – oh yes, Campbell Hall. I'll put you through.'

It seemed to take for ever but then a girl's voice answered, 'Campbell Hall, Michelle Phillips here.'

Chelsea asked for Guy. Another long pause and then his unmistakable American drawl sounded down the phone.

'Guy Griffiths here – who's that?'

'It's me, Chelsea,' breathed Chelsea, hoping her voice sounded huskily sexy.

'Who?' said Guy.

'Chelsea,' repeated Chelsea. 'Warwick's sister.'

'Oh, yeah, of course. Well, hi. How you doing?'

'Fine. Look. It's my birthday on Saturday and we're going out for a meal and would you like to come?' she gabbled, crossing as many fingers as she could manage while holding the receiver.

There was a pause. 'It's a really nice place,' she continued.

'Ah, well,' said Guy. 'It's neat of you to ask but it's kinda a long way to come for supper.' He laughed. 'And to be honest, I'm taking Michelle – my girlfriend – to a gig that night. Still, thanks for asking – have a swell time.'

'Thanks,' said Chelsea shortly. As she slammed the phone down a couple of tears trickled down her cheek. No one in the entire universe loved her.

Chapter Seventeen

Stage Directions

'Now, everyone, let me introduce our two new class members.' Miss Olive Ockley was a woman of stately build, with iron-grey hair pulled back in a bun, the bearing of a galleon in full sail and a voice which would not have been out of place reading meaningful poetry at the Albert Hall.

'This is Jemma Farrant who will be taking a number of sessions with us – am I right, Jemma?'

Jemma nodded. Her mother was still adamant that one class was enough but Jemma had every intention of cornering her father over the weekend and appealing to his better nature,

'And this,' she said, turning to a slightly built girl of about twelve with long blond hair and huge grey eyes that dominated her pale face, 'is Alexa Browning.'

Alexa smiled nervously. Jemma remembered seeing her around school – she was in the same class as Sumitha's little brother – and Jemma noted with envy that her teeth were completely even. Jemma rapidly closed her lips over her own uneven incisors.

'Now,' continued Miss Olive, hitching her ample bosom into place and beaming at the assembled class, 'as you all know, the Leehampton repertory theatre starts its summer season in March. And do I have news for you!' She paused to build up the suspense in a truly theatrical manner. 'Instead of merely asking the Olive Ockley School of Dance and Drama . . .' (Miss Olive always referred to her establishment by its full name, as if any diminution of the title would in some way diminish its standing in the community), '. . . instead of asking just for young people for the Christmas pantomime, this year they have no fewer than three productions for which they need under-sixteens.'

A murmur of excitement went round the room. The girls all began straightening their shoulders, patting their hair and trying to look nonchalant, as though the last thing on their minds was landing a part at the prestigious Royal Theatre, one of the oldest surviving reps in the country.

'The productions in question are *Great Expectations*, *Cider with Rosie* – some lovely juvenile parts there – and of course, the Christmas panto, which this year will be *Aladdin.*'

Jemma hugged herself in delight. If only she could get one of those parts, she could be famous by this time next year. It would only take someone important to spot her and she could be the next Keira Knightley. She cast an eye round the room.

She had to admit that there were several girls who were prettier than her but did they have her flair? What was it Miss Olive called it? – 'the spark'. Alexa was standing in the corner, arms crossed over her chest, looking very shy. Bit like I used to be, thought Jemma. But those days are gone; the world is going to see a new me. Next week I'll get highlights. Or maybe a silver streak.

'I have to put forward possible candidates to audition for the young Pip and for Estella within a month, so I shall be watching you all carefully,' Miss Olive was saying. 'Now, let's get started.'

The next two hours passed in a flash. The topic was 'fear' and Jemma was amazed at just how much went in to reacting fearfully to situations thought up by Miss Olive. She did quite well with facial expressions and strangled speech, but Miss Olive said that her body remained far too relaxed for someone in the throes of panic-inducing terror. Then they all split into groups and read passages from plays and took different parts.

'You go to Lee Hill, don't you?' Alexa said shyly at the end of class. 'You were Nancy in *Oliver!*'

Jemma nodded. 'Yes, that's right.'

'You were brilliant,' said Alexa admiringly. 'I wish I could act like you.'

'Oh, I'm sure you will one day when you have a bit more experience,' Jemma said condescendingly.

On the way home Jemma went to the library and borrowed *Great Expectations*. For one thing was certain; she, Jemma Farrant, was determined to be the one chosen to play Estella.

Later that evening, Rob cycled round to Jemma's house. 'How did the class go?' he asked, giving her a hug.

'Brilliantly!' said Jemma. 'And the Royal are going to do *Great Expectations* and there's going to be an audition and I want to be Estella.'

'Sounds good,' acknowledged Rob. 'Still, I suppose dozens of girls will try for it?'

'Probably, but I'm determined to get it.'

'Well, don't raise your hopes too high – after all, you've only just started,' reasoned Rob. 'You might be disappointed.'

'I thought you said I was good,' accused Jemma.

'You are – you're wonderful,' said Rob quickly. 'So wonderful I want to spend more time with you. Will you come out with me on Saturday?'

Mollified, Jemma agreed. It was nice to be appreciated.

The same evening, Jon telephoned Sumitha.

'Look, before you say anything,' he said, 'I'm sorry. Really. I honestly didn't tell anyone you were my girl-friend and I should have listened to what you were trying to say and – well, can we pretend it never happened and start again? Please?'

'As friends? Just friends?' said Sumitha, sternly.

Jon sighed inwardly. Still, anything was better than nothing. 'As friends,' he affirmed. 'How about we go out on Saturday and you can tell me all about everything. Please?'

'OK, in the afternoon,' said Sumitha.

This time don't blow it, Jon admonished himself.

Chapter Eighteen
Chelsea Breaks

By Friday, Chelsea wasn't just fed up, she was downright miserable. Normally she would have been excited about her birthday, but when the only celebration she was getting was some poxy Italian meal with her parents, and none of her friends could be bothered to come with her, what was there to look forward to? The thought of sitting over a lasagne listening to her parents trying to be hip and with it was so depressing that she was very tempted to swallow her pride and ask Jemma if she wanted to come. At least that would be one evening she couldn't see Rob.

She was sitting on the wall outside the science block, pretending she felt sick in order to miss the reproductive habits of the lesser newt, when Bex strolled round the corner.

'Hi Chelsea,' said Bex. 'Skiving off?'

Chelsea nodded.

'Want to come down town?' offered Bex, peering critically at her black varnished fingernails.

'What, now?' hesitated Chelsea. It was one thing pretending to be about to puke and quite another to get caught off-campus at half past eleven in the morning.

'Course, now,' said Bex.

What the hell, thought Chelsea.

'Yeah, cool,' she said, deliberately lapsing into Bex's speech pattern.

'We'll go out through the side gate,' said Bex, jerking her head in the direction of the football pitch. 'Less chance of being seen. I want to check out the new gear in Threadz. I've got some cash to spend – you got any dough?'

Chelsea shook her head.

'I might get some tomorrow with luck,' she said. 'It's my birthday.'

'Really? Where's the party?' said Bex, dragging Chelsea across the road to the mall entrance.

'My parents won't let me have one,' said Chelsea, looking anxiously over her shoulder in case anyone from school had seen them. 'Say it's too expensive. You know all the stuff about money not growing on trees . . .'

'So? Who needs parents to have a party? Tell you what – why don't you come down to The Tip? You know, the club next to the bowling alley? Me and Fee'll be there, I expect Trug will come and you can meet Spike, Eddie and the rest of the crowd.'

Someone wants me, thought Chelsea. And then remembered the meal.

'I'm supposed to be having a meal out at Lorenzo's with my mum and dad,' admitted Chelsea.

It sounded so pathetic – like she was some primary school kid on a special treat.

Bex raised her pencil thin eyebrows. 'Lorenzo's? Very posh,' she said.

'My dad's going to be on TV doing that *Superchef* thing and he wants ideas,' Chelsea said off the top of her head, by way of an acceptable excuse. 'I doubt I can get out of it,' she added.

Bex chewed her lip. 'We used to go out, before my dad went off,' she said wistfully. 'Anyway, why don't you come afterwards? The Tip is only round the corner from Lorenzo's.'

'I'll try,' said Chelsea, chuffed to have been asked, 'but my mum'll probably make a scene. Is yours cool about that kind of thing?'

Bex shrugged. 'She doesn't care what I do. Doesn't know half the time. Come on – let's go and try on those Capri pants – I fancy myself in fuchsia!'

I could ask Bex to come out for the meal, thought Chelsea. And then remembered her father's scathing comments about clothes and decided against it. Some birthday this was going to be.

'Where did you get to this morning?' asked Laura that afternoon as they clambered on to the school bus. 'Miss McConnell sent me to see if you were still feeling sick and I couldn't find you anywhere.'

'What did you tell her?' asked Chelsea nervously.

'I said you had gone home,' said Laura, squeezing into a window seat. 'But then you turned up after lunch. What's going on?'

'If you must know, Bex and I hit town,' said Chelsea as nonchalantly as she could.

'Bex? Bex Bayliss? What do you want to hang around with her for? She's a right weirdo.'

'She's not, as it happens. No more weird than someone who spends their time worrying about rabbits and white mice,' sneered Chelsea.

'You're getting really horrible these days, do you know that!' said Laura. 'You were foul to Jemma the other day and now you're having a go at me just because I care about animals being tortured to death in laboratories. I used to think you were really cool but you've changed. You're not the friend I knew.'

'I've changed? What about Jemma, flouncing about putting on airs and graces and going on and on about these stupid drama classes? And you? When did you last come round to my house? Oh no, it's all painting posters and sucking up to dear Daniel. You can't even be bothered to come out tomorrow night because Daddy wants you. Well, see if I care – Bex is my friend now and she knows how to have fun, which is more than you do!'

'Oh get lost,' said Laura.

Chapter Nineteen
Dads' Dilemmas

Chelsea's dad queued at the cashpoint and tried to do some mental arithmetic. If he drew out enough cash to pay for the meal and to buy Chelsea's present, there wouldn't be enough left in the account to pay the overdue gas bill or this month's Barclaycard instalment. He'd already stretched his credit card to the absolute limit getting the car serviced and he still had to get this wretched new iPod for Chelsea, the absence of which would, it appeared, bring about her instant demise. He and Ginny had rowed over that; he said it was time Chelsea learned that she couldn't have everything she wanted the moment she wanted it, and Ginny said she had to be able to keep her end up with her peer group and everyone else had them. She was feeling her way into adulthood, Ginny said; Barry wished she'd hurry up and find it.

He hated being hard up; ever since he was made redundant from Freshfoods he had been struggling. And much as he hated to admit it, this new venture wasn't exactly a moneyspinner. He wasn't losing money – but he wasn't making much either. If only he could get enough capital together to start his own restaurant – but that was just a pipe dream. The most he could hope for was that he would do well in the final of *Superchef* next month and win the ten thousand pound prize. Barclaycard would be thrilled.

The woman in front moved away and Barry decided to go for broke. He inserted his card and waited for the cash to shoot out of the little hole. Only it didn't. Instead a rather curt message saying, *We are unable to process this transaction. Refer to bank* flashed up on the screen in lurid green letters.

'I know why they use green lettering,' thought Barry cynically as he snatched back his card. 'It's to make you feel even sicker than you do already. Oh well, Chelsea, there goes your present.'

Rajiv Banerji was feeling guilty. It was Sumitha's comment that had triggered his anxiety. 'If Sandeep said he wanted to do science, you'd be telling him what a great guy he was,' she had said. Rajiv had thought about it and realised that Sandeep rarely volunteered any information at all. OK, he was too young to worry about what he wanted to do in life, but Rajiv realised with a jolt that he didn't even know what his son's favourite subjects were, who his best mates were. He never brought friends back to the house, unlike Sumitha, who at that age seemed to have half of Leehampton in her bedroom. In fact, he didn't have an inkling about what made the lad tick.

They were as different as chalk from cheese, Sumitha and Sandeep. Sometimes Rajiv thought Sumitha should have been the boy, she was more spunky, more gritty, more determined. Sandeep had never been any trouble; he was a shy, quiet little boy, small for his age, who was quite happy to stay in his room reading or making models.

But lately he had seemed even more withdrawn. Rajiv felt guilty; maybe he should spend more time with his son. He'd take him to the model shop. But not this weekend – he was on duty this weekend and had promised to show Sumitha round the new radiology unit. Next weekend. He'd do it next weekend.

Andrew Farrant removed a bright orange cardboard sun and two coat-hanger stars from his favourite armchair and flopped thankfully down. It had been a bad day; he had had seven operations to do, and little Tommy Anderson had bled badly after his tonsillectomy and was now running a high fever. He'd have to go back into the hospital later to check him over.

He pulled a tub of play dough out from under the cushion. Ever since Claire had taken on the running of this crèche, his home resembled a cross between the Early Learning Centre and an alternative art gallery and he was not at all sure he liked it. Still, he shouldn't complain; he had been nagging Claire for months to get an interest outside these four walls and he had to admit that, since she had been involved with the nursery, she had been rather less obsessed with trivia.

Not that she wasn't getting in a flap over this new drama craze of Jemma's. 'I told her she could only do one class,' Claire had said the evening before. 'I bet she comes

65

running to you and tries to get you to say she can do more.'

'Why can't she?' Andrew had replied.

'The cost, for one thing,' said Claire. 'These classes aren't cheap, you know. And anyway, she's got GCSEs looming, and you know how she needs her sleep, and anyway, she's getting very cocksure . . .'

'Getting a bit of confidence, you mean,' Andrew had interjected.

'. . . and now she's saying she wants her hair highlighted and besides, we don't know what sort of company she'll be keeping there, so we need to—'

'Hang on, hang on,' Andrew had interrupted. 'Is it the fact that you don't want to spend the money, or is it the school work, or is it the highlights? Or is it that you don't want your dear Jemma to be out of your sight for more than an hour at a time? She has a life too, you know.'

He hadn't meant it to come out so cruelly – he'd been tired.

Claire had stared at him, her cheeks pink and her eyes suspiciously bright. 'Do what you think best, then,' she'd said. 'After all, I'm only her mother.'

Andrew picked up his newspaper and sighed as he went over the conversation in his mind. At that moment, Jemma burst into the room.

'Dad, I've got a favour to ask you,' she said. 'About drama.'

'Yes,' said her father.

'You see, there are these two other classes and I wondered . . .'

'Yes,' repeated her father. 'Yes, you can do the classes – but if your school work suffers that's the end of it and no arguing!'

Jemma flung her arms round his neck. 'Dad, you're a star!' she cried. 'I will work hard, I promise – and anyway, this is really work because when I'm famous, you will . . .'

'Hang on, hang on,' said Andrew. 'You don't even know if you are going to be any good at it yet.'

'Oh yes,' said Jemma, flicking back her hair and throwing her father what she hoped was a sultry smile. 'Oh yes, I know.'

Henry Joseph surveyed his physique in the bathroom mirror on Saturday morning. Not bad, not bad for fifty-one. He pummelled his stomach in satisfaction – all this exercise was beginning to pay off. Now what he needed was a good game of golf.

'Jon!' he called. 'Jon, fancy a round of golf this afternoon, son?'

'No,' said Jon from behind his closed bedroom door. 'I'm going out.'

'With the little Indian number?' chortled Henry, slapping Macho moisturiser on to his reddened jowls.

Jon hurtled out of his room.

'With Sumitha, yes,' he retorted. 'Why do you have to talk like that? I don't imagine Mrs Banerji calls me 'the English boy.'

'No offence meant,' said Henry, holding up his hands in mock surrender. 'They're just as good as us – almost!' He tittered.

'You make me sick!' shouted Jon.

Peter Turnbull poured himself a Scotch and thought how much he was looking forward to an evening with Laura. Christmas had been a fairly disastrous event – through no fault of his whatever – and all he wanted now was a quiet chat with his daughter and a chance to get everything sorted once and for all. He'd had such a difficult year one way and another and he was feeling very fragile and stressed out. Betsy wasn't helping – he had always thought she was a compassionate, feeling sort of person but lately she had been really intolerant and snappy about his moods. And as for her children, they seemed to find fault with everything he said or did. He couldn't understand it because he had bent over backwards to be good to them. Laura had never been like that – but there again, Laura was special and he had to admit that he didn't think Betsy had quite the right approach to raising kids. He'd tried to talk to her about it but she wouldn't listen. Betsy had been rather miffed that she and her children were not included in the invitation.

'We're a family now, and your beloved daughter has got to accept that,' she had said. 'It would be a good opportunity for Sonia and Daryl to get to know Laura better.'

But Peter remained adamant. Tonight was for him and Laura. Tonight was the first stage of his master plan.

Chapter Twenty

Laura Makes a Stand

'Now look, Mum,' said Laura on Saturday morning when her mother appeared, somewhat bleary-eyed at the kitchen door. 'This is what you have to do. This box is for empty cans, this one for plastic bottles, this one's for rags . . .'

'Hang on, hang on,' said her mother, putting her hand to her head. 'I can't have all these cardboard boxes cluttering up my kitchen.'

'Oh, that's right, opt out!' snapped Laura, sticking the last label on a battered box. 'Look Mum, do you want this new baby to have a world fit to live in? I mean, think about it – think about energy and wasted resources and—'

'OK, OK,' said her mother. 'I'll make a deal with you – two boxes in the corner by the washing machine, no more. Any others will have to go in the understairs cupboard out of my way.'

'Oh yes – then it will be out of sight, out of—' began Laura.

'Laura!' said her mother

'OK,' said Laura.

'I'll be out this morning,' said Laura later while they were eating breakfast.

'Where are you off to this time?' said Melvyn. 'Some mind-extending activity like shopping, is it?'

Laura threw him a withering glance.

'If you must know, I am going on a protest.' It sounded rather good, she thought.

Melvyn and Ruth shot enquiring looks at one another.

'What sort of protest, exactly?' asked Ruth.

'Outside Leehampton Labs,' said Laura. 'Did you know they squirt shampoo into rabbits' eyes and make rats eat hair gel. It's terrible.'

'I'm not altogether sure that these protests are a very good idea,' Melvyn began.

'Says who?' sneered Laura.

'Says me,' asserted Melvyn. 'I went on a few when I was at university – anti-nuclear campaigning, that sort of thing – and half the time, they ended with some small group brawling with the police and earning the whole campaign a bad name.'

'Well, this isn't going to be like that,' insisted Laura. 'Daniel's been before and he says . . .'

'Oh, Daniel,' interrupted Ruth, sighing. 'I might have known he would feature somewhere.'

'And what's that supposed to mean?' said Laura.

70

'Oh nothing,' said her mother. 'Merely that I imagine all this recycling and sudden concern with the welfare of white mice has something to do with your crush on . . .'

Laura looked at her mother incredulously. 'What are you on, Mum? What's with all this 'crush' business? You're so old-fashioned. I have not got a crush on anyone – I just care about the world and what is happening to it. Your generation have ruined our planet and my generation have to pick up the pieces. And I am going to the demo, whatever you say!'

Ruth sighed. 'Well, I suppose . . .'

'Great. See you then.' And stuffing the remains of her toast into her mouth, she grabbed her jacket and placard and fled before anyone could stop her.

Chapter Twenty-One

It's My Birthday and I'll Cry If I Want To

'Happy birthday, sweetheart!' Ginny gave Chelsea a big hug and gestured towards the kitchen table which was piled high with parcels and cards.

'Many happys, love,' said Barry, giving her a peck on the

cheek and grabbing an earthenware cookpot from the dresser. 'I'll talk to you properly tonight – must dash – I'm marinating some rabbit over at the unit and it mustn't sit in the wine too long.'

Great, thought Chelsea. Now I come second to a dead rabbit.

Chelsea's eyes flickered over the packages and her heart sank. There was nothing there that was the right size to be an iPod, even a mini one. A tight knot of disappointment settled in the middle of her chest. Somehow she had thought that, despite all their protests, her parents would come up with the goods in the end. They always had before. Which all went to prove yet again that they didn't love her any more.

'Aren't you going to open them?' cajoled Ginny, pulling back a chair and sitting at the table. 'Look, this one is from Dad and me.'

Chelsea ripped off the paper and opened the box. There was a gold pendant in the shape of a crescent moon and a pair of gold star earrings. Wrapped round them was a cheque for twenty-five pounds. Barely enough for a pair of jeans, thought Chelsea.

'They're lovely, Mum – thanks,' said Chelsea, trying to sound enthusiastic.

'Here, let me do the clasp for you,' said Ginny, going behind Chelsea and lifting her hair out of the way. 'And look, love, I am sorry we couldn't get the iPod but things really are very tight just now. As soon as I've negotiated this rise with Hot FM and Dad's business starts to pay more, we'll think again. OK?'

Chelsea nodded. She didn't trust herself to speak.

'Open the rest of your cards, then,' encouraged Ginny. So Chelsea dutifully looked through missives from her aunt (cheque for fifteen pounds, not bad) and godmother (cheque for twenty-five pounds, even better) and grandmother (mini-rucksack, pretty cool for someone in their dotage). There was a big parcel from Geneva with an African tribal mask and a wall hanging, and a note from Warwick saying, *Happy birthday, present when I'm rich!* When she had opened the last one, she couldn't help herself any longer. She burst into tears. 'Oh, Chelsea love, what is it?' said Ginny.

Chelsea had a little sniff and said nothing.

'Oh my God, is that the time?' cried her mother, glancing at the clock. 'I'm supposed to be at a meeting for eight forty-five.' She grabbed her briefcase and looked at her sobbing daughter. Suddenly it was all too much. Whether it was frustration or maternal guilt or the fact that her column for the paper was only half written and she didn't have a worthwhile idea in her head, or whether it came from merely trying to juggle half a dozen jobs on four hours' sleep a night, she didn't know. But something inside snapped and she shouted, 'For Pete's sake, Chelsea, grow up. OK, you didn't get what you wanted, but that's life. And it's time you started realising that in the real world things don't always turn out hunky dory. I'll see you after lunch.'

Chelsea stared through tear-filled eyes at her mother's retreating backside. She'd left without even giving her a hug. On her birthday. And it wasn't fair. She wasn't crying about the present. She was crying because none of her friends, not even Laura, had remembered to send her a birthday card.

Chapter Twenty-Two

Anti-Climax

'Let's walk to the labs,' suggested Daniel. 'These placards are a bit dodgy to fit on the bus – let's see yours.'

Laura turned her placard round.

'That's brilliant!' enthused Daniel. 'You really are good with words – how do you think things up?'

Laura shrugged. 'They just sort of come into my head on their own,' she admitted. 'I'm going to be a novelist one day.'

Daniel grinned. 'You sound like my sister – she never says, "I want to be an actress," always, "I am going to be an actress".'

'Well, you have to be positive,' said Laura. 'I didn't know you had a sister.'

'Mmm, Alexa – she's twelve,' said Daniel. 'She's at your

school. She wasn't at our party – she was staying with the cousins in Sussex for the weekend.' He looked again at Laura's placard. 'Er, is that meant to be a rabbit?' he asked tentatively.

Laura pulled a face. 'Yes, but I'm useless at drawing.'

'Me too,' admitted Daniel. 'Still it's the words that matter.'

Jon draws brilliantly, thought Laura. Maybe next time, I could . . . stop it, she told herself.

'How many people are going to be at this thing?' she asked Daniel.

'Well, at least thirty from college,' said Daniel. 'And maybe some from the art college as well – and Leehampton Animal Activists probably. Hey, we cross over here.'

He slipped his hand into hers and it felt rather nice. Laura smiled at him.

By the time they reached the laboratory gates, there was quite a crowd of protesters chanting and waving placards. There were also half a dozen policemen standing chatting by the perimeter fence.

Daniel went up to a thickset guy in cord trousers and a purple anorak who was looking intently through thick-lensed spectacles at a clipboard.

'This is Laura Turnbull, she's never been to one of these before,' he said. 'Laura, this is Gavin Pykett – he's the chairman of our college animal rights group.'

'Hi, Laura,' said Gavin. 'I think you two better go over

there by the side entrance.' Gavin gestured towards a padlocked entrance. 'There's some big meeting going on this morning and we reckon the chairman of Leehampton Labs will be arriving any time. We're going to block both entrances.'

Laura and Daniel headed off and sat down on the kerbside.

'Laura – it is Laura, isn't it?' Laura looked up. Standing beside her, muffled up in a bright tangerine duffel coat and several scarves, was Jon's mum. Laura's eyes widened in astonishment.

'Hi, Mrs Joseph – what are you doing here? I mean,' she added hastily, not meaning to sound rude, 'I didn't expect to see you at something like this.'

Anona laughed. 'Why not? I get pretty incensed about all this experimentation on animals, I can tell you. So I decided to join the art college animal rights group – and here I am.'

'Brilliant!' said Laura. 'I wish my mum was that motivated.'

Anona grinned. 'I reckon if I was seven months' pregnant, I'd opt for staying at home, too. Hey, that's a great slogan,' she added, peering at Laura's placard. And with a wave she strode back to the main gate.

I wonder if Jon is here too, thought Laura, looking around hopefully. Stop it, she told herself again and turned her attention back to Daniel. He put his arm round her shoulder and she tried to fall in love.

Five minutes later, on a signal from Dave, everyone sat down. The gates were blocked with bodies four deep.

They sat there for half an hour or so. Nothing happened.

Gavin came over to them. 'Something odd is going on,' he said. 'The police aren't bothered about us sitting here – usually they are cajoling us to get up by now.'

'Can I help you, sir?' A grinning policeman ambled over.

Daniel glowered at him. Laura grinned tentatively.

'Waiting for the delegates to arrive, are you, sir?' said the constable, turning to Gavin. 'Meeting's taking place over at the company's Swansea branch. Been a bit of a waste of time for you, hasn't it, sir?'

After that it was all something of an anti-climax. Daniel was really peeved. 'Now you'll think that we're just playing at protest,' he said sulkily, 'It's a right pain this happening; I was really looking forward to a good ruck.'

Laura looked up in surprise. 'What do you mean – a good ruck?' she said.

'Oh, nothing – I just like to feel we are achieving something,' he said. 'Still,' he added, 'there's always Fettlesham Downs next month.'

'Fettlesham Downs?' said Laura. 'Isn't that the new industrial estate the other side of town?'

Daniel nodded. 'That's where CurePlan has opened its new medical laboratory. They test vaccines and new drugs and all sorts of stuff on animals and a crowd of us are going over.'

'I might not be allowed,' ventured Laura.

'Oh well, if you are going to let your parents stop you doing what you know is right, then I suppose . . .'

'No, no – I'll tell them. You're right – they have to learn. They are terribly complacent,' she added confidingly.

'Mine too,' agreed Daniel. 'It's their generation. So you are on for it?'

'Yes,' said Laura, 'yes, I'm on.'

Chapter Twenty-Three

Jon Remembers

'Mum, I'm starving – where have you been?'

Anona pulled off her scarf and hung her coat on the hall peg.

'Demonstrating at Leehampton Labs,' she said. 'You'll have to make a sandwich; I haven't been shopping yet.'

Jon sighed.

'Oh Mum – but you always used to make sausage pie on Saturdays. And you haven't made a cake for ages,' he moaned, peering into the empty cake tin.

Anona shrugged and filled the kettle.

'There's more to life than baking cakes,' she said. 'I saw

Laura Turnbull at the demo. She'd done a great placard: *Do you want beauty with no thought for the beasts?* Clever, I thought. The rabbit picture wasn't up to much, though,' she chuckled.

'Laura can't draw to save her life,' said Jon. 'I didn't know she was in to all this animal rights stuff. Mind you, give Laura something to argue about and she'll go for it.' He grinned.

'You used to see a bit of her, didn't you?'

'Mmm,' he said. She was fun, he thought. There was something fiery and fiesty about Laura. Of course, Sumitha was wonderful, no doubt about that. Still . . .

'But, of course, you're spoken for now, aren't you?' His mother smiled.

'Mum, get lost,' said Jon. And threw a wet tea towel at her.

Chapter Twenty-Four

What's in a Name?

'So how did the protest go?' enquired Melvyn as Laura walked through the door.

'Fine,' said Laura shortly. She was not about to admit that not a lot had happened and that it had been something of a waste of time.

'And everyone behaved?' persisted Melvyn. 'No nasty elements or anything?'

'Not unless you consider Jon's mum a "nasty element",' retorted Laura, hurling her coat on to the stairs.

'What's Anona got to do with it?' asked Ruth, sticking her head round the kitchen door.

'She was there, if you must know,' said Laura triumphantly. 'So you can hardly complain, can you?'

'Anona Joseph? At the demo?' Melvyn sounded astonished.

'Yes, because she happens to be a caring person who isn't content to sit at home while dumb animals are crucified for the sake of commerce!' declared Laura, feeling rather proud of that piece of vehement rhetoric.

'Well, what she does is up to her,' argued Melvyn, looking a bit taken aback. 'I'm still not really sure I approve of you going.'

'Oh, terrific!' shouted Laura. 'Well, I didn't exactly approve of you consorting with my mother or getting her pregnant, but it didn't make any difference, did it?' She threw her placard down on the hall floor and stormed off.

'Maybe it'll be different with Tarquin.' Melvyn grinned.

'I wouldn't count on it,' commented Ruth.

Laura hurtled into the kitchen. 'Who's Tarquin?' she said, throwing an empty toothpaste carton into the box marked, *Cardboard*.

'Oh, you know,' said Ruth adopting the age-old maternal technique of acting as though everything was thoroughly wonderful. 'If the baby is a boy, we are think-ing of calling him Tarquin.'

'You are thinking of doing what?' yelled Laura. 'You can't do that – it's awful! I am not going around with a brother – half-brother,' she corrected herself, glaring at Melvyn, '– with a name like Tarquin and that is final.'

'Ah,' said Ruth.

'Well, it may be a girl, of course,' suggested Melvyn. 'Then she will be called Viola.'

'Viola!' spluttered Laura. 'Viola! What are you on? Where on earth did you find a pathetic name like that?'

'I played Viola in *Twelfth Night* at school,' said Ruth.

'I suppose,' said Laura, 'we should be thankful they didn't do *Othello*. Otherwise you'd be calling it Desdemona.'

Chapter Twenty-Five

Pressure Over the Pasta

'What has she got on?' whispered Barry to Ginny as they walked into Lorenzo's.

Chelsea, who was wearing a black mesh top, red miniskirt and purple beanie, the result of an afternoon shopping on her own in town, snapped, 'I heard that –

what's wrong with it?' She hated buying clothes without her friends to back up her judgement and she wasn't at all sure about the top.

'Nothing, nothing at all,' said Ginny. 'She looks really trendy, doesn't she, Barry?' she added, giving him a deft swipe with her mock-croc boot.

'Yes, great,' he said. I'm not sure about the black stuff all round her eyes, he thought, but I suppose I'd better not mention that.

Lorenzo's was crowded with Saturday night diners but Barry had reserved a table in the far corner, under the artificial vine.

'Great for people-watching up here, isn't it, Chelsea?' chirped Ginny, who had had a long conversation with herself before they left home, applied a fresh HRT patch, swallowed some Evening Primrose oil and told herself in no uncertain terms that tonight was going to be a really good, warm, loving family evening. She knew Chelsea was upset that neither Sumitha nor Laura could join them and she wanted to prove to her that family evenings could be fun.

'So what are you going to have, love?' urged Ginny. 'You can choose anything – it's your birthday!'

Chelsea looked at the menu.

'Garlic mushrooms followed by spaghetti bolognese and a tomato and onion salad please,' said Chelsea. 'And stacks of garlic bread.'

'Oh, Chelsea,' said Barry, 'you always have that

whenever we go anywhere. This is a top Italian restaurant – why not try something different? I'm told the pan-fried liver is wonderful . . .'

'Yuck!' said Chelsea. 'Anyway, it's my birthday. Mum said I could have what I liked.'

'Sorry,' said Barry. 'Spaghetti bolognese it is. Though I still think—'

'Don't,' said Ginny through clenched teeth. 'Just don't think anything.'

'I hope you like this place, Laura, love,' said Peter, taking her arm and leading her to a corner table. 'Your mum and I used to come here years ago.'

'It's nice,' said Laura looking around. She was a bit worried. There was no sign of a parcel, no bulging pocket or discreetly hidden carrier bag. Where was her Christmas present?

'Anything to drink, sir?' asked the waitress handing them menus.

'Oh, yes, indeed,' said Peter. 'I'll have a double Scotch on the rocks and – what will you have, Laura?'

'Diet Pepsi, please,' said Laura.

'Oh yes, those were the days,' said Peter wistfully after the waitress had left. 'We'd put you to bed, Grandma would come to babysit and then we'd come here. Mum would always start with melon and parma ham, I remember.' He looked at his menu. 'You should have the canneloni abruzzi – it's got chicken livers and cream and . . .'

'I'm vegetarian, Dad, remember? I'll stick to the vegetarian lasagne.'

'Your mum's always liked that,' commented Peter, resting his chin on his hands and looking maudlin.

'Better than the weird things she's been eating lately,' replied Laura. 'If getting pregnant means eating chocolate spread and banana sandwiches, I'll pass on motherhood! Did you have a good Christmas, then?' she added, trying to jog her father's memory about gifts.

Peter sighed. 'Between you and me, no love, it wasn't that hot,' he said. 'I missed you and Mum so much, you see. Oh, thank you,' he added as the waitress delivered the drinks.

Laura was surprised. He hadn't phoned them at all over Christmas and she had assumed he was having a ball with the Bestial Betsy and had forgotten their existence.

Peter took a large gulp of his Scotch and leaned forward, resting his chin on his hands,

'Things are very difficult,' he confided. 'Sonia and Daryl — well, they just don't seem to appreciate all I try to do for them and Betsy won't hear a word against them. I sometimes feel like an outsider in their lives.'

'Well, you are,' said Laura reasonably and then hated herself for putting it so bluntly. 'I mean — well, you're not their dad, are you? Any more than Melvyn is my dad. Only to be fair, he doesn't try to take your place.'

'So I should bloody well think!' shouted Peter. 'Muscling in on my wife, my kid . . .' The carafe of water leapt alarmingly as he banged his fist on the table.

'Dad, be quiet, people are looking,' muttered Laura.

'Another Scotch – make it a double,' said Peter to the waitress.

Crumbs, thought Laura.

'I'm sorry Laura and Sumitha were tied up tonight,' said Ginny halfway through the main course. 'It must be a bore having to spend the evening with your ageing parents.'

Chelsea shrugged. 'Doesn't matter,' she said, winding spaghetti around her fork. 'I'm outgrowing them anyway.'

'And I'm sorry I've been a bit ratty lately,' Ginny went on. 'My age and all that – still, I think this HRT lark is actually beginning to take effect. This last day or so I've felt ever so much better. It's amazing – these little patches, they release oestrogen and then . . .'

'Mum!' said Chelsea through gritted teeth.' People will hear.'

'Well, what of it?' said her mother. 'So much the better if they do – it's great news for women my age, you know. The menopause is no longer something for women to merely grin and bear. I'm thinking of doing a phone-in on it next month – when I've really had time to suss it out. It's so important.'

'Well, could you contain your excitement till I'm not around?' hissed Chelsea, observing the wry grins of two women at the adjacent table,

'Pity Geneva's abroad,' said Barry, beckoning to the waitress. 'It would have been fun having her here for your birthday – always good for a giggle, our Geneva.'

I knew it, thought Chelsea; he loves her far more than me. He'd rather have her with him than me.

'Well, you won't have to put up with me for long – I'm going on somewhere after this,' she announced.

Barry opened his mouth and Ginny glared at him. He shut it again.

'What do you mean, put up with you? Darling, it's lovely to have you to ourselves for an evening. Where, exactly, are you going?' she added tentatively.

'A club – with Bex,' she said, challenging them to argue.

'Who's Bex?' said Ginny.

'What club?' said Barry.

'What is this, the Spanish Inquisition?' asked Chelsea.

'Of course not, dear,' said Ginny. 'It's just that we like to know where you are going and who with.'

'Well, Bex is a friend and the club is called The Tip and—'

'No way,' said Barry. 'Absolutely no way.'

'Pardon?' said Chelsea.

'I've seen the sorts that come out of that place at night and you are not going there and that's an end to it. And we don't know this Bex, or whatever her name is, from Adam.'

'Oh well great. Thanks a lot. I'm fifteen years old and

my father still chooses where I can go. It's not fair, everyone else's parents—'

'Look, hang on,' said Ginny. 'I've got an idea. You don't want to be dashing off tonight — we want to make an evening of it. Why don't you bring Bex home for supper one day so we can meet her, and then maybe we can reconsider this.'

'I don't believe I am hearing this!' shouted Chelsea. 'You talk to me like I'm some kid at play school – "Bring your little friend home for Mummy to vet". I'm not a baby, for heaven's sake!'

Barry and Ginny exchanged glances.

'Well, love, if this club is as bad as Dad says, I don't think—'

'Oh, forget it, I won't go,' shouted Chelsea, who truth to tell wasn't really sure she wanted to. 'I won't have a social life, I won't have any friends. Will that keep you happy?'

'Dessert, sir?' asked the waitress.

'What about a pudding, Laura?' asked Peter.

Laura shook her head.

'No thanks, I'm stuffed,' she said. She could quite happily have devoured a double portion of tiramasu, but she had watched her father demolish a bottle of claret singlehanded and she wasn't about to sit around while he ordered yet more drink.

'Oh well, then, we'll just have coffee,' he said to the

waitress. 'Oh, and I'll have an Armagnac, thank you.'

'Dad, you've had enough,' hissed Laura.

'Nonsense,' he said. 'This is a celebration. I don't see nearly enough of you, Laura.'

'And whose fault is that?' she retorted, somewhat curtly. 'You know where we are.'

'Oh, but Laura, Laura,' he began, going all misty-eyed, 'it's the agony of coming to that house and seeing your mum there with Melvyn, and now she's having a baby, and well, I simply can't bear it. I want her back, Laura. It should be my baby she's having.'

Laura stared at him open-mouthed. 'But I thought . . .'

'You see,' her father continued, 'when she decided to throw me out, I felt—'

'But, Dad,' interrupted Laura, 'you were the one who took up with Betsy.'

'Ah,' said her father, 'but you see that was because I was very vulnerable at the time – I never meant for it to lead to divorce. I explained all that to your mother. I would never have left if she had not insisted. Laura, do you think – I mean, well, is Mum really happy?'

Laura wriggled in her chair. This was getting rather too hot to handle. She didn't like seeing her dad like this. If she said Mum was happy, Dad would be hurt. But she couldn't lie either. She said nothing.

'Will you do something for me, Laura? Will you do something for your old dad?'

'What?' said Laura.

'Ask your mum to take me back,' said her father. 'Do it, Laura. Please. For me.'

Ginny and Chelsea pushed their way past the crowded tables on their way to the loo while Barry paid the bill.

'Ginny Gee!' A somewhat slurred voice accosted her.

Ginny turned to see Peter Turnbull and Laura leaving a corner table.

'Hello!' she said, taking in Peter's flushed face and slightly unsteady gait. 'Laura, how are you, love?'

'Fine thanks, Mrs Gee,' said Laura, who was actually looking far from fine. 'Hi, Chelsea.' Laura realised what she was doing there. 'Happy birthday. I've got a pressie for you at home,' she lied, 'I'll bring it to school on Monday.'

Chelsea smiled. 'Great, thanks.' So Laura did care after all.

'So this is a samily felebration – family celebration is it?' said Peter. 'Wonderful thing, families. Cherish them, Ginny, cherish them while you have them. I was just saying to my lovely Laura . . .'

'Dad!' hissed Laura, nudging him in the ribs.

This looks a mite tricky, thought Ginny.

'Well, we must be off,' she said.

'Let's walk to the car park with you,' said Peter, taking her arm in a very matey fashion.

He can't be intending to drive, thought Ginny.

Barry appeared, eyeing a till receipt with a certain amount of regret.

Ginny grabbed him. 'Offer Peter a lift home,' she muttered. 'He's had a tankful.'

'Barry – great to see you, mate, how are you?' Peter slapped Barry on the back. 'Here with your lovely family – lucky man, Barry, lucky man! The joy of family life . . .'

Laura looked close to tears. 'Dad,' she said, 'Dad, come on, please, we ought to be going.'

Chelsea looked at Peter's flushed cheekbones and unsteady gait. Poor Laura, she must feel awful.

Ginny took charge. 'Right, Peter, why don't you grab a taxi and we'll drop Laura home – you shouldn't drive, you know.'

Peter nodded sagely. 'Quite right, Ginny, wise as ever. Wonderful woman you've got there, Barry.' He turned to Laura. 'Well, goodbye sweetheart, and don't forget what I said, will you?' he added, hugging Laura. 'I'm counting on you'.

Laura nodded reluctantly and followed the Gees to the car. She felt awful – she'd never seen her father like that and she felt guilty for leaving him on his own. And what would Chelsea's mum and dad think?

'Are you OK?' Chelsea asked Laura, who was nibbling her bottom lip and gazing at the kerbstone.

'Of course, why wouldn't I be?' snapped Laura. My father forgot my Christmas present, he's turned into an alcoholic and now he wants me to talk to Mum. Oh yes, everything is hunky flippin' dory.

'Pardon me for breathing,' said Chelsea. She was fed up with people shutting her out.

Chapter Twenty-Six

Reflections in the Night

Laura didn't sleep much that night. Why did the Gees have to be at the same restaurant? She had never seen her dad like that before – he was fine when he lived with them. It was all the fault of the Bestial Betsy – she'd driven him to alcoholism. Or was it Mum's fault? Whatever, it was up to Laura to save him.

She kept going over the conversation with her father but she couldn't make sense of it. If he hadn't wanted to leave Mum, then why did he go? Or did Mum really throw him out? Laura had been told that he had fallen for someone else and was leaving. But then again, parents often told you what they wanted you to hear. But the fact remained that Dad was with Betsy, not with them and anyway, if he really cared so much about her, why had he forgotten her Christmas present? Then she felt guilty for thinking such a horrible thought. And now he wanted her to say something to Mum. Of course, it would be great to have Dad living at home again, but then, what about

Melvyn? He might be a bit of a geek but he was getting better. Besides, Mum was really happy these days. And what about the new baby? But Dad had made her promise – and she couldn't let him down. She'd have to talk to Mum. It wasn't going to be easy.

Chelsea lay awake, gazing at the ceiling. She didn't feel fifteen; she didn't actually feel anything. She knew she was pretty, certainly not thick, and fairly outgoing; so why was life passing her by? Laura had hardly said a word in the car on the way home. Chelsea guessed she was mortified about her dad being drunk, but when Chelsea had suggested that she should come over tomorrow and listen to some music she muttered about having things to do. Well, if Laura didn't want her friendship, she'd just find someone who did. She should have gone out with Bex and ignored what her parents said. After all, if she couldn't do her own thing at fifteen, when could she, for heaven's sake.

From now on, she vowed silently, pulling the duvet over her head, I shall live my life my way and if they don't like it, that's just tough.

It was to turn out rather tougher than she thought.

Chapter Twenty-Seven

Ginny Spills the Beans

'Hi, Ruth, it's me, Ginny.'

Ruth tucked the phone under her chin. 'Hi, how are you? Lovely to hear from you. You sound much happier,' she added thankfully.

'I am – it's amazing,' said Ginny. 'This last week, I've really felt like my old self again. And I've persuaded the station to devote a whole hour to a phone-in on HRT – I've got Dr Stephanie Wright coming on, and a woman from the Amarant Trust and . . . what are you laughing at?'

'You,' said Ruth, giggling. 'You get so – so enthusiastic about things.'

'Well,' said Ginny, 'I feel so much better I can't help it. I went out today and bought two new skirts and this brilliant turquoise angora sweater – now all I have to do is hide them from Barry. Anyway, what I am phoning for is . . . well, we took Chelsea out for dinner on Saturday and bumped into Peter and Laura.'

'Yes?' said Ruth.

'Well.' Ginny took a deep breath. 'Peter was a little the worse for wear with drink and I think Laura was a bit upset.'

'So that was it – she seemed very subdued when she got home.'

'Anyway, I thought I would mention it – I mean, I'm

not trying to stir up trouble or anything . . .' Ginny faltered.

'No, no. Thanks for telling me,' said Ruth. 'It's unlike him – I thought he was over all that.'

'Why? Has there been a problem in the past?' asked Ginny.

'No, not really – just that whenever he had a problem, he tended to home in on the Scotch,' said Ruth. 'Do you think I should say something to Laura?'

'I'd leave it until she broaches the subject with you,' suggested Ginny. 'After all, he didn't do any harm – it may well have washed over her.'

'Mmm,' said Ruth.

Neither of them believed that for one moment.

Chapter Twenty-Eight

Warning Signs

Everyone was very absorbed with their own concerns over the next few weeks.

Jemma had worked flat out at her drama lessons and caught Miss Olive's eye; after four weeks, she had been thrilled to see her name on the list of students to audition for Estella. Alexa Browning's name was there too (no contest, she's too timid, thought Jemma), along with a handful of other girls, none of whom Jemma rated. She had read *Great Expectations*, watched the DVD three times, started wearing her hair in coils and practised walking, talking and thinking like Estella. She had even got her own way and had two blond streaks put in her hair which, she felt sure, made her look far more sophisticated. Her mother hated them, so that was a very good sign; Rob said they were sexy, which was another plus.

'What are you looking so stuck up about?' asked Laura one afternoon, when they were changing for PE and Jemma was preening herself in the mirror.

'I'm rehearsing,' said Jemma. Miss Olive had said that to play any part well, you had to become the person you were portraying. She was busy becoming Estella.

'Well, you look pretty stupid if you ask me,' said Laura, who was not one to mince her words. 'Rehearsing for what?'

'*Great Expectations.* The Royal is doing it in the summer and I'm going to be Estella.'

'Really?' Laura was impressed. 'That's brilliant. When did this happen?'

'Well,' said Jemma, 'I haven't exactly—'

'Hey, Chelsea, wait a minute!' Laura called out across the locker room and dashed off before Jemma had time to finish her sentence. 'Guess what? Jemma's going to be in a play at the . . .' Her voice faded in the distance.

A slight niggling doubt crept into Jemma's mind. She

still had the audition to do in a couple of weeks time. Oh well, she thought, it doesn't matter. She was bound to get the part anyway. There was just one other problem. As yet, she hadn't told her mother about the audition.

Sumitha's newlyfound interest in science grew apace, although due rather more to the delectable Mr Sharpe than to any fascination with molecules and food chains. When Mr Sharpe – Paul as she silently referred to him inside her head – when Paul had asked her to help him set up a science club for Years Nine to Eleven, she was in heaven. It met on Thursdays and, if she played her cards right, she could stay behind and help clear up afterwards which gave her ten whole minutes with Paul all to herself. They were the best ten minutes of the week. Paul talked to her like an equal, discussing everything from education in India to space travel and whether she liked R.E.M.'s music, of which he was inordinately fond. He was so wonderful; she would lie in bed at night going over and over their conversations in her head. She was sure he liked her – and she knew she loved him.

'You've got a brother in Year Seven, haven't you?' Paul asked her one evening as they were packing up.

'Yes, sir.' She wanted to call him Paul but didn't dare. 'Sandeep. In Mr Bird's class.'

'Mmm,' said Paul. 'I teach him – is he OK?'

'What do you mean, sir?' asked Sumitha.

'Well, he seems very anxious all the time, rather

subdued. His written work is well above average, but he never speaks in class. I just wondered . . .'

'Oh, he's all right,' said Sumitha, put out at wasting precious time talking about her brother. 'He's just a bit wet and wimpish and he's always been shy – he'll grow out of it.'

Paul eyed her solemnly. 'Well,' he said, 'keep an eye out for him, will you? Let me know if you think there is something more to it.'

Sumitha nodded.

'At least he's got that fiesty Morrant kid as a friend,' Paul added. 'She should do him good.'

Sumitha hadn't the faintest idea what he was on about. 'Sir?'

'Victoria Morrant – pretty kid, chestnut hair, very much a live wire. Seems to have taken quite a shine to your brother.' He winked at her. Sumitha's knees dissolved.

Well, thought Sumitha, as she walked home. Sandeep has a girlfriend. How odd. How seriously sad.

The term was not progressing well for Chelsea. She'd tried getting back to the old closeness with Laura and when she bumped into her one morning, looking particularly miserable, she had asked, 'Is everything OK?'

Laura looked flustered.

'Yes, why shouldn't it be?'

'Oh, you know, I just wondered if your dad was all right, you know after that evening . . .'

'There's nothing wrong with my dad!' Laura shouted. 'So just stop sticking your nose in where it's not wanted, OK?'

'Please yourself,' retaliated Chelsea. So much for being friendly.

To make matters worse, her grades were slipping quite badly which resulted in Miss McConnell nagging her on a daily basis, Jemma and Rob were still wrapped up in one another and Sumitha had taken to spending every lunch hour in the lab or swotting in the library. The news about Jemma appearing at the local theatre had spread like wildfire and everyone was saying how brilliant it was, and wasn't she clever and perhaps she would end up on TV. How come, thought Chelsea, that Jemma gets all the breaks? She takes my boyfriend, gets a great new hairstyle that makes her look really cool and now she's going to be hogging the limelight for weeks to come. Why can't my life be exciting?

The last straw was getting caught skiving off school with Bex – the Horrific Horage had apparently been en route to the dentist and spotted the pair of them heading into the mall – Bex was a good laugh and Chelsea needed all the giggles she could get right now. After their first foray they had dodged lessons about three times a week, but then their luck ran out. Mr Horage had frog-marched them back to school and presented them to Mr Todd, the headmaster, who had droned on and on about taking responsibility and only getting out of life what you put into it, and how could they let their parents down in this manner? Bex didn't seem to care two hoots but Chelsea was worried, especially when Toddy announced that he would be writing to their respective parents.

'They'll kill me,' groaned Chelsea as they left his study, clutching their detention slips. 'What will your mum say?'

Bex shrugged. 'Nothing,' she said. 'She couldn't give a toss.'

Lucky you, thought Chelsea. I think I'll keep a low profile for a day or two.

Laura was also putting off a confrontation with her mother. She had sunk herself wholeheartedly into the recycling project and now she and Daniel were spending their evenings working on posters and banners to take on the Fettlesham demo. Laura would go next door to Daniel's house because she knew that her mother and Melvyn would kick up a fuss if they knew what she was planning; as far as they were concerned, Daniel was helping her with maths.

Then one evening, when her mother and Melvyn were out learning about panting between contractions, she had a phone call from her father.

'Hi, sweetheart,' he said, cheerily. 'How are you doing?'

'Fine, thanks,' said Laura. 'I'm doing posters for the demo.' Damn, she hadn't meant to let that slip out.

'Lovely darling,' said her father, who obviously hadn't heard. 'Now, did you speak to your mum?'

'Well, no, not yet,' she admitted.

'Laura, love, I'm depending on you,' he said imploringly. 'You see, your mum and me, we should never have split in the first place.' There was a catch in his voice. 'I want her to know that I still care, very much.'

'Why don't you tell her that, Dad?' asked Laura, who had a horrible suspicion that her father had been drinking again.

'Well, it isn't that simple, you see,' he said. 'I mean, she's got a whole lot of wrong ideas about me and she probably wouldn't listen. But if you were to speak to her, I know she'd see the sense of it all. You'd like me back with you again, wouldn't you? I mean, you do love your dad, don't you?'

'Of course I do,' said Laura emphatically. 'And of course, I'd love to have you home. Look, Dad, I have to go – I've got loads of homework to do.'

She sat for a long time thinking about her father and her mother and what had happened. Her dad sounded really odd, not like her dad at all. She knew she'd have to say something to Mum. Very soon.

Chapter Twenty-Nine

Revelations

'Read this,' said Ginny, shoving a letter under Barry's nose.

'Not now, love,' sighed Barry. 'I've got to get this hazelnut roulade right – the final's on Thursday and I'm still not convinced I've got the texture correct.'

'Damn the texture!' shouted Ginny. 'Read this!'

LEE HILL SCHOOL
From the Headmaster's office

Dear Mr and Mrs Gee,
I am sorry to have to write to you in this vein, but I have become most concerned about Chelsea. She has been playing truant from school and was found last week roaming the town centre during school hours in the company of another pupil.

In addition to this lapse, I am told by her tutors that her work has seriously declined during this term and that her general attitude is giving cause for concern.

I have given Chelsea detention for three days this week and hope that this will be sufficient deterrent to ensure that such

behaviour does not occur again. Should this
not be the case, I feel that we should meet
to discuss the whole issue.

Yours sincerely,

Michael Todd Headmaster

'I'll skin her alive!' roared Barry. 'What the hell does she
think she's playing at?'

'I think,' said Ginny, 'that she is pretty unhappy.'

'By the time I've finished with her,' stormed Barry,
'she'll have cause to be.'

'Daniel and me are going to Fettlesham Downs next
weekend,' said Laura in a rush over breakfast. She had
waited until Melvyn had left for the office, believing in the
divide and rule policy when it came to handling adults.
She didn't want another session about Melvyn's campaign
experiences.

'Daniel and I,' said Ruth automatically. 'What's at
Fettlesham Downs?'

'The CurePlan labs – they test drugs on animals.'

'In that case, no, you are not!' said her mother deci-
sively.

'Oh, that's typical – don't ask about it, don't find out
what's happening, just say no!'

'Obviously it's some sort of demonstration,' said Ruth,

'and I am sorry, but I don't want you messed up in that sort of thing.'

'Aren't you even going to listen to my side of the story?' demanded Laura.

'In this instant, Laura, no, I am afraid not,' said Ruth. 'The subject is not up for discussion.'

'Oh great – just like you never listened to Dad!' shouted Laura. 'And don't look so surprised – he's told me all about it. How you just threw him out because he was seeing Betsy, and never listened to his side of the story.'

'Hang on, hang on,' said Ruth. 'Now let's get this straight. Just what has your father been telling you?'

'The truth at last!' retorted Laura. 'How you said he had to leave because of Betsy!' said Laura. 'You didn't even give him a second chance – you just broke our family up without a second thought. And now he's so miserable that he is becoming an alcoholic and he wants to come back and I said I'd tell you.'

Ruth sat down and took a deep breath. So Ginny had been right; Laura was worried. What was worse, Laura was being used.

'I think, sweetheart—'

'Don't sweetheart me!' snapped Laura.

'I think it's time we had a little chat.' She took Laura's hands in hers. Laura snatched them away.

'Yes, you are quite right,' Ruth admitted. 'I did ask Dad to leave. He was seeing Betsy, staying away at weekends, all sorts of things.'

'But you could have given him a second chance!'

Ruth looked at Laura and smiled wanly.

'Oh, believe me, love, I had. Many, many so-called second chances. You see, Laura love, it wasn't the first time.'

'You mean,' said Laura incredulously, 'you mean, Dad had – well, had . . .'

'Dad had had several girlfriends before Betsy came on the scene. Deirdre, Judy, Belinda, Penny – oh, I lose count. After every one, he said that was the end of it and that he loved me and then – well, then he'd meet someone else who flattered his ego and it all started again.'

Laura twisted her hands in her lap.

'But when he asked you for a divorce, why didn't you just say no? Then he would have had to give Betsy up and stay with us.'

'No love, Dad didn't ask me for a divorce. I gave him an ultimatum.'

'WHAT? So it was your fault you split up?'

Ruth sighed. 'I suppose that's how it seems to you. I'd had enough of playing second fiddle to whoever took his fancy. I told him that this time he had to choose – Betsy or me. I thought that, faced with that sort of choice, he would choose to stay. I was wrong.' Ruth bit her lip.

'Why have you never told me all this before?' asked Laura.

Ruth smiled. 'I made a vow never, ever to say anything against your dad. After all, it wasn't because of you we split up. Dad worships and adores you – he always has, and . . .'

'Not enough to stay with us,' interrupted Laura, chewing her lip.

'He thought he could have it all ways – men often do,' she said ruefully. 'I kept thinking that somehow it must be my fault, that if I had been the sort of wife Dad wanted, he would never have needed to look anywhere else. Maybe if—'

'But Mum, you're worth a dozen Bestial B's,' exclaimed Laura. 'You're kind and generous and she's selfish and—'

'Hang on, hang on,' said Ruth with a laugh. 'It's sweet of you to fly to my defence, but believe me, I'm no saint. Anyway, Betsy's made your dad happy which is more than I was able to do.'

'But that's the whole point,' Laura said earnestly, 'he told me he wasn't happy; he said he wished he still had you and that the thought of you having Melvyn's baby made him really depressed. He was so miserable he had too much to drink,' she added in a whisper, torn between sounding disloyal to her father and wanting her mum to realise the seriousness of the situation.

'That must have been worrying for you,' said Ruth, taking Laura's hand. This time she didn't snatch it away. 'Sometimes people do silly things when they are feeling fed up. But I'm afraid that is something he is just going to have to come to terms with,' she continued firmly. 'I love Melvyn, I desperately want this baby and while I shall always be fond of your dad, there is no way he and I could make a go of it together now. I know it's hard for you to accept, love, but there it is.'

'It can't have been easy for you, Mum,' she said softly.

'No, love, it wasn't,' whispered her mother. 'It wasn't easy at all.'

Laura had a lot of thinking to do. She had learned things about her dad that she had never realised before. Not only had she discovered that her dad was rather weak, she had suddenly realised just how strong her mum had become.

'Chelsea, your father and I want to speak to you,' said Ginny when Chelsea arrived home that evening. 'You're late,' she added, watching her daughter carefully.

'Got talking to someone,' mumbled Chelsea.

'No, you did not,' said her father.

'You were in detention,' said Ginny, and handed her Mr Todd's letter.

Chelsea's stomach flipped. Here it comes, she thought. Here comes the 'how irresponsible can you get?' bit.

'Honestly, Chelsea, how irresponsible can you get?' began Barry.

'What were you thinking of?' asked Ginny. 'You've never done this sort of thing before. What possessed you to slope off from school?'

Chelsea shrugged and inspected her fingernails.

'Answer me when I speak to you, Chelsea!'

'It was only a bit of fun,' said Chelsea. 'Bex does it all the time – it's no big deal.'

'I consider it a very big deal,' said Barry. 'What is it with you? We never had this problem with Geneva.'

'Oh, great, that's right, throw Geneva in my face!' cried Chelsea, choking back tears. 'We all know that Geneva is your precious darling, who can do no wrong. Clever Geneva, who got a 2:1, brilliant Geneva who's working in Africa, while I'm just – well, I'm just annoying, irritating Chelsea who is in the way. The one you can't get rid of! I hate you! I really, really hate you!'

'Chelsea, for heaven's sake,' said her mother. 'That's ridiculous.'

'Chelsea, don't be silly—' began her father.

'Oh, why not? Why shouldn't I be silly? After all, according to you I'm selfish and irresponsible – I might as well be silly as well.'

Ginny grabbed her by the shoulder. 'Now look here, Chelsea,' she said, 'that's not what we're saying. All I want is for you to think about the consequences of your actions. I mean, you're a bright kid, you've got exams coming up.'

'Stuff exams,' muttered Chelsea and immediately wished she hadn't.

'Even if you don't care about your own future – and you should – you have to realise that I'm well-known in this town. If a daughter of mine is seen to be getting into bad company . . .'

'Oh marvellous. Oh wonderful!' yelled Chelsea. 'So it's not really ME you care about at all, is it? Just your precious image. All you want is to prove to the world what a fabulous mother you are, how understanding, how clued up – well, you're not. You don't understand me at all! Not one bit.'

'Now look here, Chelsea,' thundered Barry, 'don't you dare speak to your mother like that. You are grounded. For two weeks,' he added for good measure.

'That's not fair!' began Chelsea

'Life's not fair,' retorted her father shortly.

'Look, Chelsea, can't we sit down and talk this thing through sensibly,' attempted her mother. 'Just you and me.'

'No!' cried Chelsea. 'Save your patronising chit-chat for your radio show. I don't want to know. Just leave me alone!' And she rushed upstairs and slammed her bedroom door.

'Now my roulade has collapsed,' said Barry despondently.

'I think,' said Ginny, 'your roulade may be the least of our problems.'

'Jemma, please don't brush your hair in the kitchen,' complained Mrs Farrant. 'It's very unhygienic.'

'I'm seeing if I can put it in a French plait,' said Jemma. 'I've got an audition.'

'That's nice, petal. Sam, come and wash your hands for tea, please. Daniel, come out of the pedal bin.'

'It's on Saturday and you have to get me there for eleven-thirty and I need picking up . . .'

'Where for what at eleven-thirty?' asked her mother, spooning cauliflower cheese on to plates.

'Mum! You weren't listening to a word I said! I've got

an audition, for the part of Estella. At the Royal. *Great Expectations.*'

'Oh no, petal, I don't think so,' objected her mother. 'I mean, not in school term time.'

'What do you mean, you don't think so?' shouted Jemma. 'Don't you understand what I am telling you? I have been selected for an audition. Because Miss Olive thinks I am good – very good, as it happens. This is my big break and you say you don't think so! What sort of mother are you, anyway?'

Claire closed her eyes momentarily, sighed, took a deep breath and asked God for patience. 'We'll talk to Dad about it tonight,' she suggested.

'Talk all you like,' stormed Jemma. 'Talk till you're hoarse. You're not stopping me becoming a star.'

Chapter Thirty

Chelsea Rebels

'So are you coming to The Tip on Saturday?' Bex asked Chelsea as they shared a packet of crisps. 'It's a blast – much better than The Stomping Ground. And it's a special Valentine's Day set.'

'I'm grounded,' said Chelsea morosely.

'What do you mean, grounded?' asked Bex,

'Not allowed out, incarcerated,' moaned Chelsea. 'My parents flipped when they got the letter about us going down the mall.'

Bex pulled a face. 'But they can't make you – I mean, if you go out, you go out. Short of chaining you to the bedpost, what can they actually do?'

Chelsea thought about it. Bex was right. They couldn't dictate to her, she was fifteen and entitled to a life. Anyway, Dad would be sure to be out in the van so she'd only have her mother to worry about.

'OK, you're on,' she said, grinning at Bex. 'Why should they stop me having fun?'

Chapter Thirty-One

Money Worries

'Hurry up, Sumitha. Sandeep! Time you were off!' Chitrita called up the stairs and wondered for the umpteenth time that term why it was that getting two children off to school was more exhausting than teaching twenty women English grammar.

'Can I have some money for lunch?' asked Sumitha. 'And I need the money for the science trip.'

Chitrita grabbed her purse and frowned. She was sure

she had put five one pound coins in there yesterday and now there were only two. She scrabbled around in the bottom of her bag, but couldn't find them.

'You'll have to make do with this for lunch and I'll give you the rest tonight,' she told Sumitha. I must have spent more than I imagined, she thought.

'All right, you two – go!' she said, kissing the top of Sandeep's head and shoving them towards the door.

For once, Sandeep looked quite cheerful, thought Sumitha. It must be his love life.

'So how is Victoria?' she asked wickedly, as they turned the corner.

Sandeep looked at her and said nothing.

'Go on, I know all about Victoria,' said Sumitha, 'Fancy her, do you?'

'She's OK,' he muttered. How did Sumitha know about Victoria? She couldn't have said anything, could she? She wouldn't – she'd promised.

'Dear me, only OK, and there was me thinking she was the love of your life,' teased his sister.

'Shut up,' said Sandeep.

He closed his fist over the three coins in his pocket. Perhaps with those, today would be a better day.

My brother is one strange kid, thought Sumitha.

While Sandeep was putting his faith in money, Barry was staking his on his now-perfected hazelnut and cappuccino roulade.

'That's the ace up my sleeve,' he told Ginny as he prepared to leave for London. 'I just hope that, with all those studio lights, it holds its shape.'

'I'm sure it will be fine,' said Ginny. 'The best of luck. We'll be rooting for you, won't we, Chelsea?'

'Yeah,' mumbled Chelsea. And then had an idea. 'Dad,' she said, 'I'm not really grounded for two weeks, am I?'

'Yes,' said her father. 'You are.'

'I hope your flipping roulade chokes you,' snarled Chelsea.

Victoria Morrant was waiting at the school gates for her best friend, Alexa Browning, and reading *Catcher in the Rye*. Victoria had her nose permanently in a book and when she wasn't reading, she wrote jokey limericks and made cool cards for her friends. She and Alexa had been friends since they were in nursery school together and their respective mothers said they were good for each other. Victoria thought it a strange comment – carrots are good for you, early nights are good for you, Alexa is good for you. Apparently, Alexa was supposed to be a calming influence on the volatile and fiesty Victoria (who was inclined to leap head first into situations and worry about the consequences later) – and Victoria was supposed to help Alexa 'come out of herself'. Parents did say some stupid things at times. Everyone knew Alexa could come out of herself any time she liked. She was a born actress who could turn on real tears to get herself out of PE and could even go pale and do a proper-looking faint in assembly if the bribe was good enough. Victoria admired that in a friend.

Victoria was also a great champion of the underdog. Which was probably why she liked Sandeep Banerji. She got very angry with people who called him wet because he wasn't. Not at all. He was brilliant at English, top in French and very funny. Or at least he had been. Lately he had gone all quiet and solemn and hardly said a word to anyone. Then last week, she had found him crying in the cloakroom.

'What's wrong?' she had said.

'Nothing,' he had grunted.

'That's ridiculous,' she had replied, not being one to beat about the bush. 'You're crying in the cloakroom at half past eleven in the morning, so of course something's wrong. Are you ill?'

Sandeep had shaken his head.

'Well, then, what?' she had insisted.

'I mustn't – can't tell you,' he had said, and something in his eyes had stopped her asking any more.

'OK,' she'd said. 'Here – have a tissue.' He had grabbed it, rubbed at his face and headed off towards the classroom. Then he'd stopped and turned to face her.

'Victoria?' he had said. 'You won't . . . ?'

'No,' she'd said, instinctively knowing what he meant. 'No, I won't tell anyone.'

As if conjured up by her thoughts, Sandeep crossed the driveway and passed her.

'Hi, Sandeep,' she said cheerfully. 'You OK?'

Sandeep nodded. 'Hi, Victoria – I'm fine today, thanks.'

Great, thought Victoria. Perhaps it was just a flash in the pan then. I hope so for his sake.

Sandeep liked Victoria. Everyone did. He wished he was like her. She was always cracking jokes and being funny but she never made you feel bad. Not like Kevin and Matthew, who kept saying he was a puny little runt – even Sumitha called him a wimp. He hated fighting with people and he could never think of the right thing to say until it was too late. Now Kevin and Matthew were on at him all the time, calling him names and teasing him because he hated sport. But today it wouldn't be so bad.

Kevin was waiting by his locker. 'Well, little Paki boy, have you got it, then?' He was a good four inches taller than Sandeep and towered over him threateningly.

'Yes,' said Sandeep, his mouth going dry. He put his hand in his pocket and handed over a one pound coin. Kevin sneered at it.

'Correct me if I'm wrong, but I thought I said two pounds – one for me, one for my mate Matthew here.' Reluctantly Sandeep handed over another coin. 'Good,' said Kevin. 'And we'll have the same next week, thank you.'

'I can't,' said Sandeep. 'I haven't got any more.' He wouldn't dare do what he had done this morning ever again.

'Dear me,' said Matthew, clamping a hand on Sandeep's

shoulder. 'Well, I should get some if I were you. Or else me and Kevin will have to take some pretty drastic action. Eh, Kevin?'

Kevin leered and nodded.

Sandeep felt sick.

'And remember, no running to teacher. No telling tales. Because if you do, we'll finish you off. OK?'

'OK,' said Sandeep, And he didn't cry till they had gone.

Chapter Thirty-Two

Anona Makes Waves

'Just tip your head back for me, Mrs Turnbull, and we'll get you rinsed,' gushed the new junior at Fringe Affairs who gloried in the name of Amber and had obviously coloured her hair, fingernails and lips to echo her name, 'Made any plans for next summer's holidays yet, have you?'

Why, thought Ruth, wincing as the rim of the basin cut into her scalp, do all hairdressers want to know about your leisure arrangements? She was in no mood to indulge in small talk about holidays or anything else for that matter. She was too furious to be sociable.

Ruth was seriously angry with her ex-husband. He had no right to drag Laura into discussions about the breakdown of their marriage, and even less right to expect a fifteen-year-old to act as some sort of mediator between her parents.

The trouble was, she didn't know what to do. If she phoned Peter and told him what she thought, he would probably blame Laura and if she ignored the whole thing, he would simply keep on nagging his daughter to say something. She didn't want to tell Melvyn because he would lose his rag and storm round to Peter's and all hell would be let loose which wouldn't do any of them any good.

And then there was this business of the animal rights demonstration. Melvyn didn't think it was a good idea for Laura to go, but he wasn't about to stop her. He said she had to discover her own values in life and no one could do it for her. But Ruth didn't like the idea of her daughter shouting slogans and waving placards, good cause or not.

'Getting ready for a glamorous delivery, are you Ruth?' Ruth gingerly raised her head and saw Anona Joseph, wreathed in towels, smiling down at her.

'Hi,' she said. 'I thought I should have it all cut off and permed because somehow I don't think I am going to have time for hot brushes and creative flair for the next few months!'

Anona flopped down beside her. 'I'm going auburn,'

she said. 'I want a totally new image. By the way, Laura's looking well – I saw her at the Leehampton Labs demo. Nice kid, you must be very proud of her.'

Ruth nodded. 'Yes – not that I approve of all this animal rights business, though.' A thought struck her. 'What were you doing there?'

Whereupon Anona launched into an invective against animal testing which lasted ten minutes and left Ruth wishing she hadn't made a comment.

'Oh well,' said Ruth amiably, 'it wouldn't do for us all to be alike. I've just told Laura she is not to go to any more demos, especially not the one at Fettlesham Downs.'

'Well,' said Anona, 'I think you're wrong. To my mind, that savours of complacency. You should be proud that your kid has principles and is prepared to stand up and be counted.'

There is that, thought Ruth.

'I'm going – I'll keep an eye on her if that's what is bothering you,' offered Anona.

'Well . . .' Ruth hesitated.

'You can't keep her in cotton wool for ever, Ruth,' admonished Anona. 'You don't want to be another Claire Farrant, do you?'

That is very true, thought Ruth,

'Well, as long as you really do make sure she's OK,' she said.

'Of course I will,' said Anona.

Chapter Thirty-Three

Jemma's Mum Gets in a Flap

Mrs Banerji's thoughts were miles away from the class of Asian women to whom she was supposed to be explaining the rudiments of writing a business letter in English. All she could think of was the money that she was now convinced Sandeep had taken. Why? Why would he do such a thing? It was not as though they kept him short; if he had needed something, he could have asked and they could at least have discussed it.

Rajiv was all for confronting Sandeep, taking away all his privileges and going straight to the school, but Chitrita wasn't sure. There had to be a reason. She thought that maybe she would have a word with Sumitha.

At the end of class, still worrying about the problem, she headed down the corridor at the day centre and bumped headlong into Claire Farrant who was emerging from the crèche, clutching several boxes of building bricks.

'Oh, Chitrita, hello,' she said. 'I was hoping to see you. I want to ask you about Miss Olive and the drama school. I'm very worried about my Jemma right now.'

You are always worried about your Jemma, thought Chitrita to herself.

'How can I help?' she said, praying that Claire wouldn't keep her long. She needed to sort out what to do before Sandeep got home from school.

'Well, Jemma's got an audition for *Great Expectations* and I don't want her to do it,' began Claire, dumping the boxes on the floor. 'There's the school work, and then there would be rehearsals, and performances and . . .'

'Hang on,' said Chitrita. 'I thought you said it was just an audition.'

'Well, yes, but Jemma says Miss Olive thinks she will get it,' explained Claire. 'And then, of course, when I heard that Sumitha has given it all up, I wondered if that was because there was something wrong with the school.'

Chitrita took a deep breath. 'Look, Claire, Sumitha gave it up simply because she has outgrown the singing/dancing phase of her life. Miss Olive is a brilliant drama teacher but she is also just that – dramatic. She loves to believe that her students are the crème de la crème. She heaps praise on them and, in most cases, she gets the best out of them. But you have to realise there will be dozens of girls from all the other drama schools all competing for the one part. The chances of Jemma getting it on her very first attempt are, if you don't mind my saying so, fairly remote.'

'That's what Andrew says,' sighed Claire. 'But Jemma seems so confident, and she's growing up so fast, you see.'

'Well,' said Chitrita reasonably, 'she is nearly fifteen. It happens.'

'So you think I should let her do the audition?' said Claire.

'Why not? If she does land the part, then you'll have to make a decision. But I wouldn't lose any sleep over it yet.'

Chapter Thirty-Four

Ginny's Big Break

On Thursday afternoon, as Ginny was staggering through the front door, clutching carrier bags full of shopping, the phone rang.

'Ginny Gee speaking.'

'Robin Stapleton here – TV East. Ginny, we are in a bit of a tight spot and we need your help.'

'Fire away,' said Ginny, thinking that they probably wanted her to write another feature extolling one of their forthcoming costume dramas.

Ten minutes later, she put the phone down, shaking with excitement. This could be her big break. If only she could pull it off, she could be made. She ran her fingers distractedly through her hair. Keep calm, Ginny, she told herself.

'Whoopee!!' she shrieked. 'Whoopee! Whoopee! Whoopee!'

'Mum?' Chelsea appeared through the back door and gasped at the sight of her mother executing a highland fling on the quarry tiles. 'What are you doing?'

'Guess what?' cried her mother. 'Tessa Tavera – you know, *Tessa Talks* on TV East? Well, she's broken her leg filming a ski holiday piece for *The World Is Your Oyster* and they want me to front her Saturday chat show this week. And if it goes OK, I might get to cover it till the end of this series.' She hugged her daughter excitedly.

'You? On network television? This coming Saturday?' Chelsea's eyes widened.

'Yes, isn't it brilliant?'

Yes, absolutely, thought Chelsea. Now you will never find out about me going to The Tip. She pictured her mother, complete with plunging neckline and bright yellow skirt, thrusting the microphone and her breasts in the face of some long-suffering member of the audience.

'Mum,' said Chelsea

'Yes?' said Ginny.

'You will behave, won't you?'

Chapter Thirty-Five

Victoria to the Rescue

Sumitha was taking as long as she could to dismantle the science display. Mr Sharpe was standing beside her, carefully putting soil samples into polythene bags.

'Right, finished for the day,' he said, sticking on the last label.

Don't go yet, thought Sumitha.

'Tell me some more about the school in Phorabadur, sir,' she said. Anything to keep him close to her.

'Well, I don't—' Paul began, glancing at his watch.

'Sumitha! Sumitha, come quickly!' It was Victoria Morrant, panting for breath and looking very red in the face.

'I'm busy,' said Sumitha, glaring at her.

'What's up, Victoria?' asked Paul.

'It's Sandeep Banerji, sir – he's in the locker room and he's crying and he's—'

'Oh, he's always whingeing about something,' snapped Sumitha, furious that her intimate chat with Paul should have been interrupted.

'You're horrid!' declared Victoria, scowling at Sumitha. 'He's your brother, for heaven's sake.'

'Don't I know it.' Sumitha gave a mock, bored yawn, and glanced at Paul with what she hoped was a knowing look. 'It's time he grew up.'

'Sumitha, I think that is most unfair,' retorted Mr Sharpe. 'Go and check it out.'

Sumitha looked hurt. 'But sir, I haven't finished here.'

'You're brother is bleeding and you are too busy to help?' shouted Victoria. 'You make me sick!'

'Bleeding?' repeated Mr Sharpe. 'Right – I'm on my way.' And he headed off at a sprint for the locker room.

But when they got to the Year Seven locker room, there was no sign of Sandeep or his belongings.

'There you are,' declared Sumitha with satisfaction. 'He's obviously gone home. There can't be much wrong with him.'

'Well, get on home after him, will you?' said Paul. 'To be on the safe side. And Sumitha?' He paused.

'Yes, sir?' she said breathlessly.

'Try to be a bit kinder.' And he headed for the staffroom.

'I'll come with you,' announced Victoria, grabbing her rucksack and throwing her scarf on.

'I don't know what you are in such a state about,' said Sumitha, smarting at the veiled accusation from her hero, 'except, of course, that for some reason beyond my imagining you fancy my brother.'

Victoria glowered at her. 'I don't fancy him. I like him — he's my friend. And I think something is very wrong. Not that you would care. Too busy sucking up to sir, aren't you?' And with that she marched ahead of Sumitha into the school yard.

Sandeep sniffed and rubbed his nose. It had stopped bleeding but it hurt like crazy and he just wanted to go home to his mum and have a cuddle and be told everything would be all right. But it wouldn't be all right. Because Kevin had said that if he ever told anyone, he'd get sorted. And Sandeep knew what that meant.

They'd hit him because he had no money to give them. At first they had just wanted one pound each every week; then it was twice a week and now they were saying he had to give them something every day. If only he was bigger. He knew they picked on him because he was thin and small and because he wouldn't fight back.

He was just rounding the corner into Wellington Road

when Kevin and Matthew appeared from the bus shelter.

'Don't forget the cash, weedy boy,' sneered Matthew.

'And no telling tales,' added Kevin, looming over him and giving him a shove into the hedge.

'Or else,' said Matthew, kicking his shin for good measure.

Sandeep screamed, 'Stop it!' and so taken aback were they at hearing him utter a sound that, for a moment, they stopped their taunts. Sandeep broke away and ran as fast as he could towards his house.

And his scream was loud enough to reach Sumitha and Victoria who were a few hundred yards behind.

'Look, over there,' said Victoria. 'I knew it – Kevin Bott and Matthew Barnes – they've been laying into him. Come on, quickly.'

'Is that you, Sandeep?' called his mother as the back door opened. 'Good heavens, child, what have you been doing?' She cupped Sandeep's face in her hands and peered anxiously at his blood-encrusted nose.

'Nothing,' muttered Sandeep. 'I fell over at school.'

'Well, didn't the nurse clean you up?' asked Chitrita crossly. 'Honestly, it's not good enough. I shall go up there tomorrow and speak to her. You don't leave injuries like this.'

'No, Mum, please, don't go to the school, please, Mum,' said Sandeep. 'It was me – I didn't go to the nurse. I wanted to get home.'

'All right, but next time you get it seen to,' said his mother. And marched him upstairs for a session with the Savlon.

'And Sandeep,' she said, dabbing gently at his nose, 'I want to have a word with you about money.'

Sandeep gulped.

'Both Dad and I seem to have mislaid some pound coins. Do you know anything about that?'

Sandeep shook his head.

'And I found three coins in your bedroom – so what do you make of that?'

'Dunno,' said Sandeep.

'Sandeep,' said Chitrita, 'I am asking you now, and I want an honest answer. Did you take money out of my purse? Did you take cash from your father's pocket?'

'Mum! Mum!' Sumitha called urgently up the stairs.

'I'll deal with you in a minute, Sandeep,' she said grimly and went downstairs.

Her daughter was standing in the hallway with a small pretty girl who looked exceedingly angry.

'Mum, this is Victoria. Tell my mother, Victoria.'

'Mrs Banerji, I think, well, I'm sure really, although I don't actually know for sure . . .'

'Get on with it, Victoria,' urged Sumitha.

'I think Sandeep is being bullied by two boys in Year Eight,' she said in a rush. 'I don't know why, or when exactly, but I am sure it's happening. He's been so quiet and miserable and . . .' She stopped, remembering that she had promised Sandeep that she wouldn't tell anyone about seeing him in tears.

So that's it, thought Chitrita. But why hadn't he said anything to her? She was his mother, for heaven's sake.

'Come in and sit down, Victoria,' said Chitrita. 'And thank you, thank you for telling me. Sumitha, did you know of this?'

Sumitha looked rather shame-faced. 'I knew he'd been whingeing a lot,' she said defensively. 'But I'm not his keeper.'

'No, you're his sister!' snapped Victoria. 'It was obvious something was wrong, but you were too busy swooning over Mr Sharpe.'

Sumitha threw her a thunderous look.

'Well, you were,' mumbled Victoria.

'Mum, what's . . .' Sandeep appeared at the sitting room door and stopped dead when he saw Victoria.

'Sandeep, Victoria has told us everything,' said his mother gently.

'But Victoria, you promised,' said Sandeep. 'You promised.'

Victoria looked crestfallen.

'I didn't say anything about that,' she assured him.

'You are very lucky to have a friend like Victoria,' said his mother, putting an arm round his shoulder. 'And don't worry, we are going to get this whole thing sorted out.'

'But don't tell Kevin and Matthew,' blurted out Sandeep. 'They said they'd beat me up.'

Chitrita's eyes filled at the thought of her son's anguish.

'You don't have to worry any more,' she said. 'Everything is going to be all right.'

Chapter Thirty-Six

Fathers in a Fix

'I'm back!' Barry called from the front door.

'Guess what, Barry,' said Ginny rushing downstairs in a green face pack and scarlet kimono.

'What?' said Barry flatly.

'I've been asked to front the *Tessa Talks* show on Saturday – and I might get the rest of the series. Isn't that sensational?'

'Great,' said Barry.

'Oh, sorry, love, I forgot,' said Ginny. 'How did it go? Did you win?'

'I'm not supposed to say till transmission date, but who cares? No, I didn't win.'

Ginny felt her heart drop to her kneecaps.

'Oh, love, I'm sorry.' She didn't know what else to say.

'Don't be. I'm obviously not good enough. In fact, I'm not good for much, am I? Good thing we have you to hog the limelight. I'm going to have a bath.'

And with that he plodded dismally upstairs, leaving Ginny feeling both deflated and guilty.

'So that's about the strength of it,' said Chitrita to Rajiv that evening. 'Sandeep has been bullied and used the money in an attempt to buy the bullies off.' She was close to tears.

Rajiv put his arm around her. 'What can we do? I must go to the school,' he said. 'Poor kid, what he must have gone through. Why didn't he tell anyone? Us? Or Sumitha?'

'I think he tried to.' Sumitha appeared at the doorway looking miserable. 'It's partly my fault. Dad – he kept asking to walk with me, and asked me to give him money and I just teased him. I never stopped to think why he was doing it. Now I feel dreadful.'

'I think,' said Rajiv thoughtfully, 'I have an idea. And it might just work.'

Chapter Thirty-Seven

The Best Laid Plan

Saturday morning saw a hive of activity in several Leehampton households.

Melvyn was rushing around like a scalded cat looking for some folders.

'I'm sorry, love,' he said to Ruth, 'but I have to go into the office. The system has crashed and old Stockton is having kittens.'

Ruth sighed. 'So you can't come to the supermarket, then?' she said, wearily thinking about humping six boxes of groceries from the trolley to the car on her own.

'No, but Laura'll go with you, won't you, Laura?' Laura looked up from her magazine.

'I can't – I . . .' she began and stopped. She had every intention of going to the demo somehow, but she wasn't about to get nagged at again.

'Your mother is seven and a half months' pregnant, for heaven's sake,' said Melvyn. 'The least you can do is help her. Must dash – see you around teatime.'

Laura slammed the magazine on the table.

'So are we going, then?' she said, less than charmingly.

'No, it's all right, I'll manage,' said her mother. 'You can go to the demo with Daniel. Not that I really approve mind,' she added hastily. 'I'm only letting you go because Jon's mother said she would keep an eye out for you.'

Laura was so ecstatic that she didn't even point out that she needed no one looking out for her.

'I think,' her mother added ruefully, 'that it might be best if you don't say anything about this to Melvyn. He seems to think I am the first woman in the history of evolution to have a baby.'

'I won't,' Laura assured her, as she gave her a hug.

'Do take care!' called Ruth to Laura's retreating back. But Laura had gone.

'Are you coming to the airport to meet Gran, Jemma love?' asked her mother, poking her head round Jemma's bedroom door. 'Her flight gets in at one o'clock.'

'Of course I'm not!' snapped Jemma, waving a mascara wand in the air. 'It's the audition – I told you.'

Claire sighed. She had forgotten about this wretched audition.

'Well,' she said, 'I'll drop you off there but you will have to make your own way home. I can't be late for Gran.'

Jemma shrugged. 'You could fetch me on your way back – then I can tell Gran the news.'

'I think,' commented Claire, 'that after a fourteen-hour flight, she may have higher priorities than hanging around in a theatre waiting for you.'

'Suit yourself,' said Jemma.

'Barry! Telephone!' Ginny laid the receiver on the hall table and grabbed her suitcase. 'I'm off, love,' she said as her husband appeared in the doorway. 'Do I look OK?'

'Fine,' said Barry, taking in Ginny's white bouclé dress which sat on her hips like an uncooked meringue, 'but what's with the suitcase?'

'I thought I should take a few outfits – you know, see what the producer wants.'

There's hope for the viewing public yet, thought Barry. 'Good luck,' he said. 'See you later.'

He picked up the phone.

'Barry Gee,' he said.

'This is Will Zetland,' said a deep American voice. 'You don't know me, but I have a proposition I would like to put to you. Can we meet?'

'I feel like death,' groaned Mrs Joseph, gulping down two spoonfuls of cold remedy. 'I'm going back to bed.'

'I thought today was the big demo,' said Henry, flexing his muscles in the mirror.

'It was but I feel too ill to move,' said his wife. 'Oh heck, I was supposed to be keeping an eye on Laura Turnbull. I suppose I should phone.' She picked up the bedside phone and punched in Ruth's number. There was no reply.

'I'll do it later,' she murmured and crawled under the duvet.

Downstairs, her son was flicking through the local paper. I'll take Sumitha to a movie this afternoon, he thought, and then a pizza and then we'll come back here and . . . He quivered with anticipation of what might follow.

Trouble was, he didn't want his dad around if he brought Sumitha back.

'What are you doing today, Dad?' he called through the study door.

'Eighteen holes with Richard Garrett,' replied his father. 'Then on to the club for a few beers.'

Great, thought Jon. After a quick calculation over the cost of his carefully thought out programme of seduction, he added, 'Dad? Can you lend me a tenner?'

Chapter Thirty-Eight

Tempers Flare

By the middle of Saturday afternoon, Laura was cold, fed up and disenchanted. They had come across town in the college minibus, full of hype about the day ahead.

CurePlan had just marketed a new drug to deal with respiratory problems and the rumour was that it had been tested on a variety of animals. Someone had discovered that the TV programme *Health Matters* would be filming at the lab that day and Gavin Pykett was beside himself with excitement.

'This is our chance,' he told everyone as the bus trundled across town. 'I want plenty of noise, placard waving, and do make sure you sit in ranks on the approach road.'

After four hours of sitting on the approach road, Laura had nothing to show for it except a red nose and numb bum. The TV crew had arrived at midday, disappeared into the main building and still not reappeared. There was no sign of Jon's mum and Daniel had spent most of the afternoon with his nose in a book. Even the duty police officers looked bored stiff.

'I'm cold,' she complained to Daniel. 'Let's go home.'

'Oh terrific,' snapped Daniel, 'Laura's chilly so the campaign's off. Hey, what's happening?'

Just then a TV cameraman emerged from the building, together with an interviewer and two grey-haired men in pinstripe suits. They stood on the forecourt and began what was obviously an interview in front of the camera.

'Right!' shouted Gavin. 'Let them have it!' And suddenly, everyone was rushing to the perimeter fence, clambering over, waving placards, chanting slogans and running full pelt towards the camera crew.

'Come on,' cried Daniel, grabbing Laura's arm. 'This is it.'

Several policemen had leapt into the fray and were pushing people back from the fence.

'This way,' shouted Daniel and ran round to the side of the building. 'Through here.' From his duffel coat pocket he produced a pair of wire cutters and began pulling at the fence.

'Daniel, we can't – we mustn't,' protested Laura. 'It's illegal.'

'Since when did that matter?' snapped Daniel and wriggled through the fence. 'Coming?'

Laura hesitated. Several people had started throwing

stones and other missiles, others were grappling with policemen. Laura wished she had never come.

Daniel began running towards the forecourt where the cameraman had turned his attention from the CurePlan executives to the scuffle in front of him.

Laura watched in horror as Daniel hurled himself on one of the grey-haired men.

'Murderer!' she heard him shriek. He drew his arm back, fist clenched.

'Daniel, Daniel, don't!' Laura began running after him. He'd be arrested at this rate. She had to stop him.

Suddenly she felt an agonising pain on her left temple and fell to the ground. She put her hand to her head and to her horror it came away covered in blood. Then the grass began to wave and dance before her eyes. It started to turn brown, then black. And after that, Laura remembered nothing at all.

Chapter Thirty-Nine

Very Great Expectations

Jemma walked home from the audition on a real high. She had been brilliant, she just knew it. The producer had called her back three times and asked her to read different passages. She could see the admiration in his eyes, that same look as Rob gave her every time she had run through the part with him. He had called her 'Jemma, my love', which she knew was what theatrical people did when they were smitten with you.

Of course, Alexa had been called back as well, and two other girls from the Selby Drama School. But Jemma was absolutely certain she had got the part.

'You will be hearing via your own drama teachers within a week or so,' the producer had announced at the end of the auditions. 'The standard was very high – thank you all for coming.'

Now she was going to dash home, phone Rob and get him to take her out to celebrate. I bet his mates will be so envious of him, having an actress for a girlfriend, she thought delightedly. That's one up on Chelsea and Laura and everyone.

Jemma opened the front door and called out, 'I'm back'.

'In here, petal,' replied her mother and so elated was Jemma that she didn't even protest.

In the sitting room, Gran was ensconced on the sofa and beside her was a balding, grey-haired man with sun-wrinkled skin.

'Hi Gran,' said Jemma, 'did you have a good time?'

'*Ni hao*, Jemma,' said Gran. 'That's Mandarin for hello. Yes, wonderful, amazing, fantastic. Oh, and this is Tom – Tom Keen.'

'Hello,' said Jemma. 'Gran, I am positive I got the part.'

'Part, darling?' asked Gran.

'Estella,' said Jemma.

'Estella?' said Gran.

'Mum, haven't you even told Gran about the audition? About how good I am at drama? Mum?'

Claire looked at Jemma.

'No dear, I haven't,' she said.

'Well, thanks a bundle,' shouted Jemma. 'Gran, I've been—'

'And the reason I haven't is that Gran has some very important news. Far more important than yours, I might add.'

Jemma was about to protest that nothing was as important as her impending stardom, when Gran interrupted.

'As I was saying, dear,' she said, 'this is Tom. My fiancé. We are to be married in six weeks' time.'

Chapter Forty

More Grief for Jon

It had all been so easy with her mother out at the TV studio, and Dad suddenly announcing that he had to dash to meet some guy she had never even heard of, Chelsea had enjoyed bags of time to get ready for her night out with Bex.

She'd drawn out money from her savings account – which she wasn't supposed to do without permission, but who cared? – and bought this brilliant orange A-line miniskirt and a skinny T-shirt that showed off her curves. She piled her hair on top of her head and spent ages getting her make-up just right. Tonight was going to be good.

Jon's Saturday, on the other hand, was not going as planned. He and Sumitha had gone to see the latest Spielberg film which had been great, except for the fact that, whenever Jon had tried to put his arm round Sumitha, she pointedly removed it. The most he'd got to do was hold her hand, and she'd kept taking that away to feed herself popcorn.

Then they had gone for a pizza.

'You know,' he said, 'I really, really like you.'

'That's nice.' Sumitha smiled. 'I like you too. Can I ask you a favour?'

'Of course,' said Jon. Anything, anything.

'Well, you're a guy,' she began.

'Yes,' said Jon.

'Well, I've got . . . I've got this friend and she really loves this guy, but she isn't sure how he feels about her. Should she ask him outright or just keep quiet and wait to see what happens?'

Oh wow, thought Jon. It's not a friend really. It's her. She really loves me and is scared to say so.

137

'Oh, she should definitely say something. Without doubt, the sooner the better,' gabbled Jon.

'You think so?' queried Sumitha. 'Really?'

'Really,' insisted Jon. 'Absolutely.'

'Right,' said Sumitha. 'That's what I'll . . . that's what I'll tell her to do.'

Jon waited. Nothing happened.

I'll take her home – she'll tell me there, he thought.

They went to his house, ate chocolate chip cookies and drank Coke. Sumitha told him about how she was going to do science at Birmingham University.

'Why Birmingham?' said Jon.

'That's where Paul went,' said Sumitha and bit her tongue.

'Paul?' snapped Jon.

'Mr Sharpe, our science teacher,' explained Sumitha. 'He is the most amazing, incredible person you have ever met in your life.'

I'll kill him, thought Jon.

'Talking of science,' said Sumitha. 'Would you do something for me?'

'Of course,' said Jon

'I'm stuck on question four of my biology homework. I've brought it with me. Can you take a look?'

She proffered her science book. Jon sighed. This wasn't quite what he had in mind. Still, at least it kept her with him for a bit longer.

The back door opened and Jon's father staggered in under the weight of his golf bag.

Oh no, thought Jon. Why does he have to come back early?

'Well, hello, Semelda,' Henry boomed.

'Sumitha,' corrected Sumitha.

'What are you two up to, then, huddled up together? Or shouldn't I ask?' Henry winked at Jon who cringed with embarrassment.

'Jon's helping me with my biology,' explained Sumitha.

'I wouldn't have thought a pretty little thing like you needed to worry her head about matters scientific,' said Henry.

Sumitha bit her tongue.

'I'm going to be a scientist,' she said.

'Really? Well, well. I thought you people tended to go into the family business and that sort of caper. What's your father do? Run a Balti house?'

'No, Mr Joseph, he does not. He is a radiologist at the General. My mother is a teacher of English. Jon, I have to go. Thanks for looking at that, but my father is bound to be able to sort it out for me. Bye.'

And without a backward glance she walked out the door.

'Dad,' said Jon, 'you are the pits.'

Chapter Forty-One

Trouble at The Tip

The Tip was amazing. It was all decked out to look like the town dump, with oil drums as tables and sawn off logs and upturned rubbish bins as seats. In one corner was a huge artificial rubbish heap made out of polystyrene on which an assortment of kids lounged. Hanging from the ceiling were old dustbin lids, hub caps, ancient lawnmowers, wringing machines and all sorts of paraphernalia.

'So you came then?' Fee had commented when Chelsea turned up. She was wrapped around a guy with an orange Mohican and a long leather jacket. 'Spike, this is Chelsea – mate of Bex.'

Spike inclined his head infinitesimally by way of acknowledgement.

'Sex-eeee!' A tall, thickset guy with a crew-cut leaned across Bex and said, 'I'm Eddie. Want to dance?'

As they tried to move on the packed floor, which was littered with empty crisp packets and cigarette ends ('It's all part of the scene, they never clear up,' Eddie explained), Chelsea looked round her. Most of the kids were older than her and a lot of them were drinking. The air was heavy with smoke and she began to feel a bit uncomfortable. Still, Eddie seemed very friendly and even Fee seemed to have accepted her.

In the middle of the dance floor, Eddie held her tight against him and began kissing her. She pushed him away. It didn't feel right – she hardly knew the guy.

'Don't, please – no,' she gasped.

'Oh dear, dear, going to be a little tease, are you?' Chelsea shrugged him off and headed for the corner where Fee and Bex were lighting up cigarettes.

'OK, Chel?' Bex appeared at her side. 'Want a fag?'

Chelsea shook her head.

'I expect Mummy doesn't like diddums to smoke,' sneered Fee. So much for the new-found friendliness, thought Chelsea. She looked at Bex for support.

'Go on, have one,' she urged. 'Everyone does.'

'Maybe you'd rather have one of these instead?' Eddie waved a handful of white pills at her. Chelsea gaped.

'No, I wouldn't!' she said.

'They're harmless,' said Eddie, pushing one towards her. 'Honest – just make you feel good.'

'No way,' she said.

'Leave her, Eddie,' said Fee. 'She's only a kid – she can't handle it.'

Chelsea had had enough.

'I have to go, anyway,' she said. 'Bye, Bex.'

And she pushed through the crowd and out on to the pavement and began heading up the hill to the bus stop.

Suddenly she heard someone coming up behind her.

'Hey, don't run off now,' said Eddie grabbing her arm. 'I've got plans for us.' And he pushed her into a doorway and began kissing her, running his hands over her bottom. He smelled horrible and Chelsea was scared.

'Don't,' said Chelsea, pushing him away. 'Don't do that.'

'Oh come on, now,' he said. 'That's what you've been angling for all evening. Don't be the prissy little miss with me now.'

He grabbed a handful of hair, tipped her head back and began kissing her neck. His fingers fiddled with her bra strap. Chelsea screamed, kneed him swiftly in the groin and ran like hell up the road, tears pouring down her face.

Chapter Forty-Two

A Shock for Ruth

'I want to watch Ginny on that chat show,' called Ruth from the kitchen. 'OK if we eat on our laps?'

'Fine by me,' said Melvyn. 'Where's Laura?'

'Er, out with a mate,' said Ruth. 'Should be back any time now.'

In fact, she was rather late, thought Ruth. Still, knowing Anona, she had probably invited Laura back for tea.

They settled down with their plates of lasagne in front of the TV.

'And now, before Tessa Talks, *we are going over to the news-room for an announcement.'*

Andrea Goodson, TV East's head newscaster, appeared on screen.

'Reports are coming in of a major disturbance at the CurePlan laboratories at Fettlesham Down, just outside Leehampton.'

There was a clatter as Ruth's fork hit the plate.

'Police in riot gear were called in to break up protesters who broke through the perimeter fence during the filming of an episode of Health Matters.'

'What did I say?' commented Melvyn. 'It happens so often. Still, thank heaven Laura got that particular bee out of her bonnet. I wouldn't have wanted her in the middle of all that.'

Ruth's heart was racing. She knew Laura was there. A clip of film was being run on the screen,

'Several people were arrested, and two people, including a teenage girl, were injured during the incident and were taken to Leehampton General Hospital. We will bring you further . . .'

'Oh, my God!' Ruth cried. 'Look! It's Laura! Oh, my God!'

The camera panned to two paramedics lifting a teenager into an ambulance. As they stood back to close the doors, Laura's white face, eyes closed, was clearly visible.

Melvyn's face blanched. Ruth grabbed his arm.

'What in the name of . . . OK, keep calm – I'll phone the General. Get your coat.' He paused. 'Do you think the Brownings know?'

Ruth was crying too hard to reply.

'I'll run round and tell them. Don't worry, love, she'll be OK.'

A few minutes later, Alexa Browning opened the front door.

'Is your mum in?' asked Melvyn.

'No, I'm afraid she and Dad have gone out. Gran's here, though.'

An elderly lady with an anxious expression came to the door. 'We thought you should know – our daughter, Laura, was with Daniel this afternoon at a demo at—'

Alexa's gran held up her hand. 'I know. That's where Rodney and Barbara are now – at the police station. Sorting out my hot-headed grandson. Oh, my goodness – that girl on the television – that wasn't—'

One look at Melvyn's grim expression showed that it was.

'We're on our way to the hospital now,' he said shortly. 'We'll discuss all this with Daniel later.'

Chapter Forty-Three

Chelsea Seeks Shelter

Chelsea ran until she had such a bad stitch that she had to stop. She looked warily over her shoulder, but there was no sign of Eddie. She took out her mobile and rang home.

'Hi, thank you for calling the Gee family. No one is available at present to take your call . . .'

Sugar. Dad was obviously still out and she knew her mum wouldn't be back for at least another hour.

'Please speak clearly after the long tone.'

'It's me, Chelsea,' she began and started to cry. Then her phone started beeping and switched itself off. Chelsea realised that, with all her evening focussed on getting ready, she had forgotten to charge it. As she was trying to get it to turn back on, a guy passing by gave her an odd look. She pocketed her phone and fled.

She felt sick. Everything had turned out wrong. She thought she was going to have a brilliant evening and make new friends and instead of that she'd made a total idiot of herself. What was it with her? She'd really hated it when Eddie had come on strong, but surely at fifteen she should be enjoying a bit of a snog?

She didn't want to walk home in the dark. That would be asking for trouble. She thought she would get a taxi but she didn't have enough cash. She would have to wait till she thought Dad was back and get him to pay the driver.

She was shaking, partly with cold and partly with misery. Across the road she saw the lights of The Fishbone fish and chip shop. She'd get a coffee and then try ringing home again.

She peered into a shop window, rubbed her smudged mascara ineffectually with a paper tissue and went into the shop.

Chapter Forty-Four

Casualty of War

It seemed to Ruth as if they would never get to the General. Every traffic light was red, every roundabout clogged with traffic.

Why had she listened to Anona? Why had she let Laura go? What had happened to her? She couldn't tell from the shot on the television how badly hurt she was.

'Why on earth did Laura go to that wretched thing in the first place?' said Melvyn, tapping his fingers on the steering wheel as they sat in yet another queue of traffic. 'I thought she was out shopping with you most of the day.'

'Actually,' whispered Ruth, 'I went on my own. I said she could go.'

'You did what?' yelled Melvyn. 'You shouldn't be doing all that on your own at a time like this, and besides I specifically told Laura she couldn't go.'

'Anona Joseph was going and said she would keep an eye out for her, and I thought it would be all right,' she said.

'Oh wonderful,' said Melvyn. 'So now Laura is in hospital with heaven alone knows what sort of injury and—'

'All right, all right, you don't have to go on!' shouted Ruth, trying very hard not to cry. 'I'm feeling bad enough without you laying into me!'

'Hey, don't get upset – you've got the baby to think of,' said Melvyn.

He sped into the hospital forecourt and pulled up outside Accident and Emergency.

They ran up to the reception desk. 'My daughter, Laura Turnbull – she's been brought in – she was in the Fettlesham demo.'

'Oh yes, Mrs Turnbull. If you will just take a seat, I'll get someone to have a word with you.'

'But how is she? Is it serious?'

'Just take a seat, and someone will be with you directly.' The nurse smiled soothingly.

Within a few moments, another nurse bustled up to them, carrying a chart.

'I'm Staff Nurse Nisbet,' she said. 'You can see Laura now. She's doing fine. She was unconscious for a few minutes – hit by a stone, we think – but she came round very quickly. We've had to give her four stitches, but it's under her hairline and there's no great damage done.'

'Thank God,' said Ruth and burst into tears.

Laura was lying on a trolley in one of the curtained cubicles. She was very pale and had a big sticking plaster on her left temple. When she saw her mum, she began to cry.

'It was awful, Mum – really scary. I tried to stop Daniel, and then something hit me and now the police have taken Daniel and—'

Ruth wrapped her arms round her.

'It's OK, sweetheart, it's OK now,' she murmured. 'We're here.'

Chapter Forty-Five

Surprises on the Small Screen

Chelsea wrapped her hands round her mug of coffee and shivered. She felt miserable and alone and scared. She was about to drink the rest of her coffee and try calling from a phonebox when she heard something that made her look up in surprise.

'And now will you please welcome your host for tonight – Ginny Gee!'

There was a burst of applause from the TV set mounted above the fish bar. And there was her mum, looking surprisingly elegant in a taupe silk shirt and cinnamon pants, smiling to camera.

'This is the show they call Tessa Talks *– only tonight, it's me, Ginny Gee, who is doing the talking and hoping that you, the audience, will join me in discussing a topic close to many of our hearts – teenagers.'*

Here we go, thought Chelsea.

'She's good, that Gee woman,' said a man behind her to his companion. 'She does Hot FM and writes in the paper – really cool stuff. My wife swears by her.'

Despite herself, Chelsea felt quite chuffed. She decided to order another coffee and watch the show.

'Chelsea? Are you OK?' Bex flopped down on the seat beside her. 'I've been looking everywhere for you.'

Chelsea looked at her. 'I suppose you think I'm totally

uncool,' she muttered.

Bex shook her head. She looked really worried.

'I think you're brilliant,' she declared. 'Eddie had it coming to him – he tries it on with everyone. And . . . I'm sorry,' she added.

'What for?' asked Chelsea. 'You didn't do anything.'

Bex shrugged. 'That's the point. I didn't. I guess I should have warned you – it was Fee's idea. She thought it would be a laugh to make you look stupid so she set the whole thing up. She didn't reckon with you being so sassy. Hey, isn't that your mum on telly?'

Chelsea nodded and glanced at the screen. A member of the audience was asking a question.

'Do you have teenagers of your own? And, if so, how do you maintain a good relationship with them? I suppose in your line of business you have all the answers.'

Chelsea groaned inwardly. 'Let's go,' she said to Bex.

'No wait, let's hear what she says.'

'Well, I have a lovely fifteen-year-old daughter, a nineteen-year-old son and another daughter in her twenties. Of course, I adore them all.'

'Only she likes Geneva best,' muttered Chelsea.

'And, as for having all the answers, if only I did. The point is, you see, that none of us have. Take me: my youngest daughter is a delight but she's going through a rough time right now. Drifting apart from her long-standing friends, grappling with growing up, and on top of everything, having to cope with a menopausal mother.'

149

The audience laughed sympathetically.

'I never knew she realised,' murmured Chelsea in surprise.

'*So how do you handle it all?*' persisted the questioner.

'*All you can do is love them, unequivocally and all the time. You may not always like what they do: but you must let them know you are there for them.*'

'*Yes, but what about when they are rude and rebellious and just downright, well, maddening,*' said another woman. '*Or is your kid a saint?*'

'*Far from it!*' said Ginny, smiling. '*She drives me insane at times – but then, I understand I have the same effect on her – wearing the wrong clothes, saying the wrong thing to the wrong person at the wrong time – being parental in fact!*' Another laugh.

'*But despite all the aggro, deep down I know she is there for me, just as I am always there for her. I'm just dreading the day when she grows up and leaves home – but I try not to think about that.*'

'I wish my mum was like that,' said Bex softly. 'I reckon you're so lucky.'

'Me too,' said Chelsea, sniffing, and hoped Bex wouldn't see that she had tears in her eyes. 'I'm going home.'

'Chelsea?' said Bex. 'We can still be friends, can't we?'

'Of course,' said Chelsea.

'Good,' said Bex.

Chapter Forty-Six

Shocks on Screen

Jon sat slumped in front of the television. Some Saturday night this had turned out to be. He couldn't believe how his dad had behaved. Even his mum had been pretty shocked when he related the conversation. He was sure he'd lost Sumitha now. Not that she had turned out to be as much fun as he had expected. Hard work was one thing, but she never seemed to want to laugh or joke around. Maybe they just weren't cut out for one another. Maybe he would never ever have a girlfriend. Maybe he was just a freak.

'Switch the local news on, Jon, there's a dear.' His mother staggered into the room in her dressing gown, clutching a pile of tissues. 'I want to see if there's anything on about the demo.'

Ten minutes later, Anona was sitting, head in hands, riddled with guilt. 'I forgot all about phoning Ruth,' she wailed. 'If that kid on the TV was Laura, she'll never forgive me. Jon, do you think it could have been someone else?'

Jon didn't reply. He was heading out to the General Hospital.

Chapter Forty-Seven

Parental Panics

Ginny turned the key in the front door. She was walking on air. The producer had been delighted with the show and booked her to cover for Tessa until she was out of plaster.

'Chelsea! Barry! I'm home,' she called.

Bother, she thought. I want to share this with someone. She ran upstairs and knocked on Chelsea's door. 'You awake, Chelsea? Can I come in?'

She pushed the door open. The room was empty.

And so was the rest of the house.

Ginny had run the full gamut of emotions, from fury with her daughter for going out without permission when she was grounded to the tearful certainty that she had been abducted, run over by a truck or rushed to hospital with appendicitis.

'The answerphone!' she thought and played back the only message recorded.

'It's me, Chelsea . . .'

Thank heaven. Ginny waited. There was the sound of stifled sobbing and then an ominous click. And nothing.

'Oh my God!' cried Ginny to the empty house and was about to phone the police when Barry arrived home.

'Ginny – great news! Our troubles are over! You—'

'Barry – it's Chelsea; she's not home and on the answer-phone, she said "It's me," and then nothing.'

Barry stopped in mid flow. 'What do you mean, nothing?'

'What does nothing usually mean?' she snapped. 'She started to leave a message and then it all went dead. Oh God, Barry, suppose someone's—'

'Now hang on, love. Let's think this through. Have you tried her mobile? Phoned Laura's house? Sumitha's?' suggested Barry.

Ginny told him that Chelsea's phone went straight through to voicemail, then duly phoned around. There was no reply from Laura's, and the Banerjis assured her that they hadn't seen Chelsea for weeks.

'I'll take the car and go and look for her,' said Barry. 'You don't suppose she might have gone to that Tip place, do you?'

'Maybe,' said Ginny, 'I'll come with you.'

'No, you stay here in case she phones,' said Barry.

But as they opened the front door, a cab pulled up outside. Chelsea tumbled out and flew up the path and straight into her mother's arms.

'Chelsea, thank God – are you all right?' Her mother choked back tears of relief that her daughter was in one piece.

'I'm sorry. Mum, I . . .' Chelsea was sobbing too hard to speak.

Barry paid the taxi driver while Ginny led Chelsea into the house.

Ten minutes later, the three of them were seated round the kitchen table, drinking mugs of cocoa.

'Now tell me, sweetheart, and tell me truthfully, did this Eddie do anything other than try to kiss you? No one will be cross, but you must tell us.'

'No,' said Chelsea, shaking her head. 'I kicked him in the crotch.'

'Good for you,' said Barry. 'And you didn't take that pill?'

'Of course not,' said Chelsea indignantly. 'Give me some credit.'

'If I ever get my hands on him . . .' muttered Barry. 'Not that you should have been out anyway, you were grounded,' he added sternly. Frankly he was so relieved to have her home safe and sound that he had almost forgotten to be cross.

'I know. I'm sorry. I just felt that since no one cared anyway, there was nothing to lose.'

'But darling, of course we care,' began Ginny.

'I know that now – I saw the TV show.'

'Oh, I forgot – how did it go?' said Barry.

'Fine, but we'll talk about that later,' said Ginny. 'What were you saying, darling?'

'I went to the fish and chip shop and your show was on the TV and when that woman asked about your kids, you said you loved me and didn't want me to leave home and I thought you hated me and loved Geneva best and couldn't wait to get rid of me,' said Chelsea in a rush, tears spilling over once again.

'Oh, sweetheart – how could you think that?' cried Ginny. What sort of mother was she? How could she not have made it clear that Chelsea was everything in the world to her?

'But Dad said he wished Geneva was home,' said Chelsea.

'I did?' said Barry, looking puzzled.

'That night at Lorenzo's,' she said.

'Oh – well, that was just because I reckoned it would be much more fun for you. You must miss Geneva – you and she used to be really close.'

Chelsea nodded. 'I do miss her,' she said, acknowledging the fact to herself for the first time.

'What else?' asked her mother gently.

'And you were cross about my room, and Dad hated my clothes and none of my friends seem to want me around . . .'

'Sweetheart, listen,' said Ginny. 'We want you, very very much. Sometimes we let our personal worries and disappointments and anxieties spill over into our relationships – I do it with your dad, he does it with me. That's life. It happens. I look at you and I see this stunning, gorgeous girl and I think – help. Please God, don't let her go off the rails. Or get hurt. Or be anything other than happy. And then I go too far the other way and come over the heavy-handed mum.

'We both love you very much,' said Barry. 'Come to think of it, I could name the new restaurant after you. Chelsea's. Nice ring, don't you think?'

'What new restaurant?' chorused Chelsea and her mum.

'Ah well, that's my bit of news. I had a call from this guy, Will Zetland, who saw me on *Superchef*. He's bought the old Famished Friar restaurant in Bridge Street – you know, the one that closed down last spring – and he wants me to run it. He'll do all the business side and give me a free hand with the food. And I get a salary,' he added, winking at Ginny.

'Fantastic!' cried Ginny. 'Oh Barry, I'm so happy for you!' She jumped up and gave him a big hug.

'Dad, that's brilliant!' said Chelsea. 'But don't call it Chelsea's – please. That would put my mates off me even more.'

'Oh well, you'll have to think up another name,' said Ginny, making a mental note to talk to Chelsea about the whole subject of friendship.

'What's this other guy's name?' said Chelsea.

'Will Zetland,' said Barry.

'There you are then,' said Chelsea. 'Gee Whizz. You're Gee, and his initials are W.Z. Gee Whizz.'

'Chelsea,' said her father, enveloping her in a bear hug. 'You are one amazing kid. Gee Whizz it is.'

Chapter Forty-Eight

Jemma Faces the Music

'But Gran – you can't get married!' exclaimed Jemma for the tenth time that day.

'Oh, I rather think I can, sweetheart,' said Gran equably. She turned to Tom, who was gazing at her adoringly, and squeezed his hand. 'I think we shall make out rather well, don't you, my love?'

'Quite admirably,' said Tom, smiling at her. 'And to think, I shall have a ready-made granddaughter to spoil.' He grinned at Jemma, who tossed her head and looked away. 'And Jemma dear,' continued Gran, 'I'd like you to be my attendant at the wedding – first Saturday in April.'

'Oh, sorry, if it's a Saturday I shan't be there – I shall be rehearsing,' said Jemma. 'Estella is a very important role.'

She was very miffed that her Gran was more concerned about getting married than her granddaughter's impending fame.

'I wasn't aware that you had actually got the part,' interrupted her mum 'and if you have we still have to discuss whether you will take it.'

Jemma raised her eyebrows impatiently. 'Well, I haven't actually been told I've got it yet,' she admitted. 'But it's pretty obvious – I was easily the best one there.'

After her grandmother and Tom had left, Jemma rounded on her mother.

'Well, aren't you pleased?' she snapped.

'Delighted, darling – Gran deserves to be happy.'

'Not about Gran, about me and the part,' said Jemma irritably.

'Not really, no.'

Jemma stared at her open-mouthed.

'Anything that threatens to turn you into a self-opinionated, smug little madam, who is too wrapped up in herself to be happy for anyone else, is not likely to give me pleasure,' said her mother. 'And if you do get the part, I am not at all sure that you will be allowed to take it.'

Jemma was so taken aback she forgot to close her mouth. Her mother was looking at Jemma with real distaste. And what was more, she hadn't once called her petal.

Chapter Forty-Nine

Laura Receives a Tonic

'I think you can take this young lady home now,' said the doctor gently, laying a hand on Laura's shoulder. 'And steer clear of crowds – we don't want you taking any more knocks for a few days. Now, if you could just sign this . . .' He turned his attention to Laura's mum.

'I suppose you think I got what I deserved?' Laura said

to Melvyn as her mother signed the doctor's forms. 'You never wanted me to protest in the first place, did you?'

'It's not the protesting that worries me, love,' said Melvyn. 'I admire you for having principles and feeling strongly enough to do something about them. What I cannot stand is the way some people seem to think that violence is the answer to everything – if someone doesn't agree with you, hit them first and think afterwards. That's the philosophy that sickens me.'

Laura smiled wanly. 'Don't worry, I'm going to stick to writing books from now on,' she said. 'Do you know what happened to Daniel?' she asked, as they walked through the waiting area to the main entrance.

'Apparently he was taken to the police station,' said Melvyn grimly. 'I'll be having words with that lad later on.'

'Oh, don't go and make a scene!' pleaded Laura. 'It'll go all round the school if Alexa hears about it. It was as much my fault as his – if I hadn't tried to stop him . . .'

'You tried to stop him making a complete idiot of himself,' said Melvyn. 'He's older than you; he should have known better.'

Laura sighed. She hadn't really expected Daniel to be such an idiot. Protesting was one thing but Melvyn was right; getting violent and abusive was something else altogether.

'Laura! Laura!' She turned round, wincing slightly at the pain in her head. And blinked. Twice. Perhaps the bang on her head had been worse than they thought. She could swear that was Jon, leaning on the nurse's desk.

'Well, Jon, fancy seeing you here!' said her mother as he came towards them. So she wasn't dreaming. It really was Jon. 'Oh, dear, is it your mother? Was she hurt too?'

Jon shook his head. 'She's got the flu, so she didn't go,' he said. Ruth was about to say something pointed about irresponsibility and bit her tongue. After all, it wasn't Jon's fault.

'Are you all right?' he said, glancing anxiously at Laura's white face and plastered forehead. 'Did you break anything? I came as soon as I heard.'

Laura shook her head, and winced again. 'No, I just got cut on the head – I'm fine,' she assured him. 'But how did you know I was here?'

'I saw it on the TV,' he said.

'I was on television?' asked Laura, perking up.

'On the local news,' said Jon. 'It really panicked me – you looked, well, I thought you were . . . so I came.' He blushed and fidgeted with his scarf.

'Well, we must get Laura home,' said Ruth briskly, noticing that her daughter was looking rather bright-eyed and flushed and thinking she might be running a fever.

'Er, would it be all right if I came round tomorrow?' said Jon. 'Just to see how you are?'

'Well, she's supposed to rest,' began Ruth.

'Yes,' replied Laura firmly. 'That would be great.'

She was feeling better already.

Chapter Fifty

Love for Laura

'I bought you these,' said Jon when he arrived at Laura's house on Sunday afternoon. He handed her a box of Quality Street.

'Thanks ever so much,' said Laura. Her stomach was turning over and she didn't think it was an after-effect of the accident. 'And thanks for coming yesterday,' she added. 'That was really nice of you.'

'That's OK,' said Jon. 'I did this too.' He handed her a sheet of paper, covered with cartoons. 'It's a sort of history of the times we've met. It struck me that there always seems to be some sort of crisis when I see you,' he added with a grin.

There was Laura hurtling down the hill on her bike months before, Laura lying in a heap at Jon's feet, Laura trying miserably to draw pictures, and Laura, head bandaged, looking battered and bruised.

'It's brilliant!' she said. 'We do seem to get together in odd circumstances, don't we?' she added, thinking silently that it was worth having an aching head if it meant getting Jon to herself for a while.

'Yes, well,' said Jon, taking a deep breath. 'I mean, we could change that. I mean, I was thinking – well, I kind of think you are really cute and – will you go out with me?'

Damn, he thought. That sounded so naff. How uncool

can you get? Laura was staring at him, open-mouthed. He'd blown it. He knew it. He should have been more laid back.

'I'd like that,' said Laura.

'You would?' asked Jon.

'Very much,' said Laura, smiling.

Chapter Fifty-One

Birth Pangs

'You sound very cheerful,' remarked her mother on Monday morning, interrupting Laura's rendition of Madonna.

'I am,' said Laura.

'Would this have anything to do with Jon's visit yesterday afternoon?' asked her mother, smiling.

'It might,' admitted Laura.

'Well, it's good to see you happy,' said her mother, giving her a hug. 'But I really don't think you should go to school today – you still look a bit pale and that cut hasn't had a chance to start healing.'

'Oh Mum, I'll be fine, honestly. Don't fuss,' said Laura. She had to go to school to tell everyone – including Sumitha – about her and Jon. She felt like she was walking on air. It was true what they said: being in love was the most wonderful thing in the whole world.

She was gathering up her kit when she heard a scream from the kitchen.

'Laura! Lau–raaaah!'

She rushed downstairs to find her mother hanging on to the door handle, clutching her stomach. The floor was rather wet.

'Laura – it's the baby. It's coming!' Ruth gasped.

'But it can't be – you said it wasn't due till March the twelfth,' protested Laura.

'Well, it obviously doesn't have a calendar in there,' snapped Ruth. 'Sorry, love. Look, can you ring Melvyn's office and . . . aaah!'

'Sit down, Mum,' said Laura firmly, leading her mother into the sitting room. Heart pounding, she phoned Melvyn's office.

'I'm sorry, Mr Crouch has gone over to our Kettleborough office,' said the telephonist. 'Can our Mr Leadsom help you?'

'Not unless he has a diploma in midwifery,' said Laura acerbically. 'Can you phone him and tell him my mum is in labour?'

'Oh, my goodness – oh well, yes of course,' said the girl. 'At once.'

Laura went back into the sitting room.

'This isn't meant to be happening,' gasped Ruth. 'The contractions – they're coming really close together.'

'I'll phone for an ambulance,' said Laura. 'Just don't give birth on the floor. Please.'

Chapter Fifty-Two

Now We Are Four

'He's so little,' breathed Laura, leaning over the cot in the Special Care Baby Unit. 'He is going to be all right, isn't he?' she added.

'The nurse said he's doing really well,' said Melvyn reassuringly. 'That's right, isn't it?' he added, turning to the nurse who was adjusting one of the tiny tubes attached to the baby.

'He's doing brilliantly,' she said. 'You were just a bit too impatient to come into the world, weren't you, little one?' she said to the baby.

'The mother had had some sort of shock, I understand,' said another nurse who was attending to a tiny baby in the next cot. 'That probably induced premature labour.'

It was my fault, thought Laura. If I hadn't gone to the demonstration and ended up in Casualty, Mum would never have had the baby early. If the baby dies, it'll be because of me.

'Come on, let's go upstairs and see your mum,' said Melvyn.

'Have you seen him? Isn't he adorable?' Ruth asked as Laura gave her a kiss.

Laura nodded. And burst into tears.

'Laura, love, what is it?' asked her mother anxiously. 'You'll get used to having the baby around.'

'Mum, I didn't mean to make this happen,' she said. 'He looks so little, and he's got tubes and things in him and—'

'Laura, love, listen,' said Melvyn quickly. 'He's going to be fine. Honestly. The nurse explained. With premature babies they take precautions. He's only four weeks early and that's no big deal. And there's this new drug they use which helps their breathing. He really will be just fine. It's wonderful what modern medicine can do.'

Laura wiped her eyes. 'I'm so glad that Charlie's going to be OK.'

'Charlie?' chorused Ruth and Melvyn.

'Well,' said Laura, pulling herself together, 'you didn't seriously believe I was going to let you call him Tarquin, did you? Besides, I've always thought of it – him – as Charlie. Charles for a boy. Charlotte for a girl. Charlie.'

Ruth and Melvyn exchanged glances. 'Charlie,' mused Melvyn. 'It has a ring to it.'

'Charlie,' repeated Ruth. 'I like it.'

'That's settled then' said Laura.

Chapter Fifty·Three

Bad News for Jemma

Laura was, not surprisingly, the centre of attention when she went back to school on Tuesday. Her friends had heard about her accident and they wanted to find out all the details.

'I was a fool,' she said honestly. 'I thought Daniel had it all sussed, about this protesting and stuff, when all the time what he was looking for was a fight. I reckon he would have demonstrated against anything – just for the sake of it.'

'What happened to him? Were his mum and dad mad at him for getting arrested?' asked Jemma.

'Pretty much, I think,' said Laura. 'The police sent him home with a caution and I know his dad has said he can't have any driving lessons for six months.'

'Tell us about the baby,' said Chelsea. She desperately wanted to get back to being friends with Laura again.

'He's cute,' she said. 'He's unbelievably tiny with dinky little fingernails and a button nose. I don't suppose,' she added hesitantly, 'you'd like to come to the hospital with me after school, to see him? I mean, if you're busy with Bex or something . . .'

'I'd love to come,' said Chelsea. 'Really love to.'

'Do you want to come, Jemma?' asked Laura.

'Can't, sorry,' said Jemma. 'It's drama class and I need to find out the rehearsal schedule for *Great Expectations*.'

'Oh,' said Laura. 'Are you still in it? I assumed you wouldn't be now, what with Alexa getting the part of Estella.'

Jemma stared at her. 'What did you say?' she demanded.

'Alexa Browning – didn't I say? Oh well, when Daniel came round to apologise last night, he said that Alexa had just had a phone call to say she'd got the part of Estella. I thought he'd got it wrong because you said you'd got it,' she added, slightly puzzled.

'Of course he got it wrong,' thundered Jemma. 'There is no way that kid could have got the part. I was tons better than her. There's been a mistake. I'm sure there has.' She rushed off towards the pay phones.

Chelsea looked at Laura.

'Whoops,' they said in unison.

Close by, Sumitha took a deep breath and went up to Mr Sharpe's desk. She slipped the envelope into his folder. Then, heart thumping, she took her seat and waited for class to begin.

Chapter Fifty-Four
Baby Talk

'He looks just like you did when you were born,' said Ruth to Laura as they leaned over Charlie's cot on Tuesday evening. Ruth had been discharged but Charlie had to stay in the Special Care Baby unit for a few more days. 'You are pleased, aren't you, Laura?'

Laura nodded. 'I think he's cute,' she said. 'I rather like being a big sister.'

She sighed.

'What is it, love?' asked her mother.

'Oh, I was just thinking about Dad,' she said. 'I mean,

you're happy, and I just wish he was too. I want you both to be happy.'

Ruth squeezed her hand.

'I know, love,' she said. 'But you have to remember something. It is not your responsibility to make either of us happy. You mustn't feel that just because Dad is going through a difficult time, it is somehow your fault. It's not. No way.'

'But he wanted me to get you to let him come home and, even though I can see now that it wouldn't work, he'll think I didn't even try.'

Ruth shook her head.

'No,' she said. 'I've written to Dad. A letter just between the two of us. I've told him how I feel and I've also asked him not to put this kind of pressure on you again. And don't worry,' she added, 'I've told him how much you love him.'

Laura felt like a weight had been lifted from her shoulders.

'Thanks, Mum,' she said. 'You're cool, you know that? Oh look, Charlie's been sick.'

Sumitha hung around in the locker room until everyone had left. Then she went back up to the science lab.

Paul was sitting on his desk, thumbing through a pile of essays. He looked up as she walked in.

'Ah, Sumitha,' he began.

'Sir – Paul,' she gulped. She'd done it. She had said it. 'Did you read the card I left for you?'

'I did, Sumitha,' said Mr Sharpe, putting down his papers and turning to face her. 'And before we go any further – before you say things which one day you will feel embarrassed about, or I start preaching and sounding like that agony uncle guy in *Shriek*, let me tell you what you already know, deep down.'

Sumitha stared at him. Was he going to tell her that she was his favourite, that he realised she wasn't a stupid kid, that he . . .

'I am your teacher, I am twelve years older than you and any idea that you may have of loving me is merely a crush. I'm sorry if that sounds harsh, but it's true.'

'No – I do, I think you're amazing,' protested Sumitha. 'You're a brilliant teacher.'

'Thank you,' said Paul. 'But never forget that is all I am. Your teacher. Nothing more. And now, I must lock up. Good night, Sumitha.'

Chapter Fifty-Five

Jemma Exits the Stage

Jemma lay sprawled out on her bed, crying her eyes out. It just wasn't fair. How could Alexa Browning – who was only twelve! – be chosen to play Estella, while she, Jemma

Farrant, whom everyone knew had bags of talent had been totally ignored? How was she going to face everyone? She'd been so sure of getting the part that she had told all her friends that she would get them tickets – and now she wasn't even going to be the understudy.

Nobody seemed to realise how awful it was. When she had phoned Miss Olive, all she had said was, 'There will be plenty more parts to play, Jemma, and Alexa just had the right Victorian look about her.' Her mother just said, 'It won't do you any harm – you were getting far too big for your boots,' and Gran, who had been so keen on her doing drama in the first place, had remarked, 'Disappointment is very good for the young,' which Jemma thought was a pretty useless sort of thing to say.

Even Rob hadn't understood.

'There'll be other plays,' he had said when she sobbed down the phone to him. 'And besides, it means we can spend more time together and actually talk about something other than drama. You were getting altogether too taken up with this acting lark anyway.'

'Fat lot you know!' she had said and slammed down the phone.

But deep inside, she knew what was hurting most of all. It was the fact that she had told everyone she was bound to get the part. She had kept going on about how good she was – and the fact was, she obviously wasn't. If she had been, she would be playing Estella instead of Alexa.

She used to think that if she was outgoing and confident and bubbly like Chelsea, she would have stacks of friends. Well, she had tried it. And now, she probably wouldn't have a single friend left in the whole world.

Chapter Fifty-Six

Bullies Brought to Brook

'I've just seen your dad going into Mr Todd's study,' said Laura to Sumitha on Wednesday morning before assembly. 'What's going on?'

Sumitha chewed her lip, 'Well, don't tell anyone, but it's about Sandeep. He's been bullied.'

Laura looked aghast. 'That's awful – what happened?'

'I'm not supposed to say anything about it until Mr Todd has sorted it,' she said. 'I just feel so awful that I never realised what was going on. Sandeep's been so miserable for so long – and I just told him to grow up.'

'Don't worry,' said Laura, laying a comforting hand on Sumitha's shoulder. 'Your dad and Toddy will get it sorted.'

'I hope so,' said Sumitha. 'I do hope so.'

Behind the closed door of the headmaster's study, Matthew Barnes and Kevin Bott were standing, eyes downcast, in front of the desk.

'This,' said Mr Todd, 'is Mr Banerji. Sandeep Banerji's father.'

Kevin shuffled uneasily and Matthew bit his fingernails.

'Good morning, Matthew. Good morning, Kevin,' said Mr Banerji politely extending his hand. They each shook it rather half-heartedly.

'Mr Banerji would like a word with you,' said Mr Todd.

The boys looked apprehensive.

'Now then,' said Rajiv. 'I assume you are both going to taunt me, tease me, ask me for money and then, eventually, should I be foolish enough to stand up to you, you will hit me. Well now, time is short; you have an assembly to attend so I suggest we get on with it.'

Matthew and Kevin stared at him.

'You are puzzled? Have I got it wrong?' asked Mr Banerji. 'Is this not the way you behave?'

They said nothing. Matthew twisted his hands behind his back and Kevin chewed his lip.

'Is this not the way you behaved towards my son? And indeed, he is no different from me. We are both Bengali. Our skin is not white, it is brown. And we are both people who like a quiet life – we hate to make waves. So why are you not bullying me right now?'

'It was no big deal – just a bit of fun . . .' ventured Kevin.

'Oh, I see,' said Mr Banerji. 'So hitting small boys in the dark corners of the locker room, and extorting money from them when they think no one is looking is your idea of fun? You know, I feel so very sorry for you both.'

The boys looked at him in surprise.

'You are surprised?' queried Rajiv. 'Oh yes, I do feel sorry for you. Because to act in that cowardly, low-down sort of way you must both be very unhappy boys. I hope that you and your parents and Mr Todd can sort this whole dreadful business out because I would not like to think that anyone, including you, has to go through life feeling as miserable as you made my son feel. That is all I have to say,' he added. 'What happens now is up to Mr Todd.'

The headmaster stood up.

'To me, and to Year Eight,' he amended. 'The class will hold a bully court next week and we shall endeavour to sort this whole thing out. Thank you for coming, Mr Banerji, it is much appreciated.'

Sumitha caught up with her father as he was leaving the building.

'Dad, what happened? Is it going to be all right?'

Her father smiled wryly. 'All right? Well, hopefully Kevin and Matthew will be helped to see the error of their ways and, between us, we must try to restore Sandeep's self-respect and confidence.' He sighed. 'But it is up to all of us, whatever age, to be on the lookout for this sort of thing. And, if we see it, to have the courage of Victoria and do something about it. The problem was that Sandeep was afraid to tell anyone; he should have come straight to me, or his mother, or you – it would have saved him so much pain.'

Sumitha nodded. 'And if I had listened to him, instead of always nagging at him, he just might have felt able to tell me,' she said tearfully.

Half an hour later, Mr Todd was addressing the school assembly.

'And now for two pieces of happy news. Firstly, our congratulations to Alexa Browning of Year Seven, who has been chosen to play Estella in the Royal Theatre's forth-coming production of *Great Expectations*.' He paused while the applause rang out. Jemma bit her lip.

'Bad luck,' said Chelsea touching her shoulder, 'Never mind, there's always next time. You're really talented – you'll make it.'

Jemma looked at her. She thought Chelsea would be delighted that she had messed up.

'And Jemma,' whispered Chelsea, as the applause died down, 'can we be friends again? I'm sorry I was such an idiot over you and Rob.'

Jemma smiled. 'Yes, please – I missed you.'

'Me too,' said Chelsea.

'And lastly, I am delighted to announce that Mr Sharpe, our new science teacher, has become engaged to Miss McConnell.'

Chatter broke out in the room and some smart alec called out, 'Fast work, sir.' Sumitha gulped. Paul. Paul was

174

getting married? He couldn't. She loved him so much. How could he fancy mousy Miss McConnell? How could he?

Well, if that was his game, she was certainly not going to give up any more Thursdays to organise his rotten science club.

'Can Victoria come to tea?' Sandeep asked his mother that evening.

'I think that would be a great idea,' said Chitrita.

'Sandeep's in love,' teased Sumitha.

Her mother glared at her. She didn't want Sandeep's newly found confidence bruised.

'You can talk,' retorted Sandeep. 'Anyway, Mr Sharpe's getting married so you won't be able to swoon over him any more!'

'Get knotted,' muttered Sumitha, but she grinned at him while she said it.

Sandeep stuck his tongue out and grinned back.

Well, well, thought Chitrita. Things are taking a turn around here.

Chapter Fifty-Seven

Gee Whizz!

Excitement was mounting in the Gee household as the opening of Barry and Will's new restaurant approached. It was attracting a great deal of publicity, thanks to some careful orchestration by Ginny, who managed not only to get the local newspaper to devote three-quarters of a page to the enterprise, but persuaded Hot FM to run their weekly *Food Fanatics* slot from the kitchen.

When the decorators finally moved out, Barry suggested to Will Zetland, who was an entrepreneur with a finger in a number of extremely lucrative pies, that they should throw a private party the evening before the official opening. 'It will give our friends a chance to see what we are doing and it will be a good practice run for the staff,' explained Barry.

'Can my friends come too?' Chelsea asked, thinking that a free meal would be a good way of getting them all back together again like before.

'Of course,' said her father. 'What I'd really like,' he added tentatively, 'would be for you and some of your friends to come along for the grand opening as well and hand round canapés and give out leaflets. But of course, if you think that would be a naff thing to do . . .' Barry was very anxious not to ruffle the newly calm atmosphere in the household.

'That would be great,' said Chelsea. An idea hit her. 'Dad?' she said.

'Yes, sweetheart?'

'Can I have some money? I've absolutely nothing to wear for such an event.'

Some things, thought Barry, fishing out his wallet, never change.

Chelsea and her mum went on a mammoth shopping spree during which Ginny, who had recently celebrated the effectiveness of her HRT by acquiring a perm and a chestnut rinse, lashed out more money on a new purple suit and a waistcoat in a rather interesting shade of banana. Chelsea used her father's cash donation to buy a pair of faded-denim hipsters.

Then they had coffee and doughnuts and a long heart-to-heart talk about friends and love and the meaning of life in general.

'Have you seen any more of your friend Bex?' asked Ginny hesitantly.

'Only at school,' said Chelsea. 'She told me she's stopped going around with Fee and that lot.'

'I was just thinking that you should invite her over sometime,' commented Ginny.

'But I thought she was the sort of person you didn't approve of. Dad certainly didn't.'

'Well, it just seems to me that she cared enough to follow you that night and make sure you were all right.

From the little you have told me, it sounds like she might not be a very happy kid. As long as you bear in mind that old adage that your granny used to chant – make new friends, but keep the old . . .'

'. . . for one is silver, the other gold,' finished Chelsea, grinning. 'I know – Jemma's coming round after school tomorrow. We're friends again. I reckon it's not worth losing a mate because of a boy.'

Ginny grinned. 'You're learning,' she said.

Life in Laura's house was a little more frenetic.

'When is this kid going to learn that you sleep at night and stay awake in the day time?' yawned Laura at three o'clock one morning, when Charlie was making it perfectly clear that he needed food and he needed it now.

'Bless him, he's only three weeks old,' protested Ruth, warming a bottle.

'Jon wants to draw his portrait – if he ever stops yelling long enough, that is,' said Laura.

'Things going well with you two, are they?' enquired Ruth.

Laura chose not to reply. She didn't want to tempt providence. She leaned over Charlie's cot and tickled his toes.

He grinned.

'Mum, Mum – he smiled at me!' cried Laura.

'Wind, darling,' said her mother. 'They don't smile until they are six weeks old.'

'No, he smiled,' insisted Laura. 'He's obviously a very advanced kid. He gets his brains from his sister.'

Ruth smiled. She had an idea that Charlie had a champion for life.

'Jemma! Telephone!' called Claire.

Jemma galloped downstairs and snatched the receiver.

'Rob? Oh, oh sorry. Hi, Miss Olive. Pardon? Yes. What me? Really? In the summer? Oh wow! Thank you. Thanks a million. Yes, see you on Saturday. Bye!'

She hurled the receiver back on the cradle and flew into the kitchen.

'Mum! Mum! You'll never guess what! That was Miss Olive and Jake Huntley, that's the man producing *Great Expectations* – well, he just—'

'Jemma, Jemma, calm down. I can't understand a word you're saying,' said her mother, laughing.

Jemma took a deep breath. 'The producer of *Great Expectations* is going to do *Cider with Rosie* in the summer. And he wants me for the part of Marjorie! It's a great part – I can do it, can't I Mum?'

'Well . . .' began her mother.

'Please?'

'You won't get all big-headed and stroppy with us?' said Claire, eyeing her sternly.

'Sumitha, can I say something?' Victoria Morrant was waiting for Sumitha at the school gate.

'Yes, of course,' said Sumitha. 'Sandeep's OK, isn't he?' she added anxiously. 'I mean, there hasn't been any more trouble?'

Victoria shook her head. 'No, he's fine. I'm just waiting for his football practice to finish, then he said I could come to your house for tea. Which is why I just wanted to say that I'm sorry I was rude and yelled at you that time. I know it wasn't your fault but I was worried and didn't know what to do.'

'Hey, hang on,' said Sumitha. 'If anyone should be saying sorry, it should be me. I was so wrapped up in myself I didn't take any notice of my brother. I mean, he can be a mortal pain at times, but I should have sussed out that something was wrong. I'm glad he had you rooting for him.'

Sandeep came rushing up, red-faced and out of breath.

'Hi, Victoria,' he said. 'Er, Sumitha, you're not going to walk home with us, are you? Puh-leese!'

Sumitha grinned. 'Touché,' she said.

Chapter Fifty-Eight
The Final Course

'I've got a brilliant idea!' enthused Barry on the morning of the opening gala.

'Could you have it quietly?' pleaded Ginny, who was suffering the effects of a surfeit of champagne at the party the night before.

'Listen, Chelsea,' he said, ignoring his wife. 'How would it be if you and your friends dressed up in berets and striped T-shirts for this evening? You know, have a French theme?'

Chelsea gave her father a withering look.

'Dad, get a grip – that is such a cliché! Really pathetic,' she protested.

'Oh,' said Barry.

'Besides,' she continued, 'I've got my new hipsters and Laura's getting some wicked flared jeans and Jemma reckons she can con her mum into buying her a fluffy angora jumper because she'll say it keeps the cold out!'

'Oh, well,' sighed Barry. 'Even if the restaurant flops, I will have kept retail sales in the clothing industry at an all-time high!'

Chelsea giggled. 'It won't flop, Dad,' she said reassuringly. 'Everyone said the food was way amazing – and you know Jemma's gran has chosen Gee Whizz for her wedding meal. Hey, you might even get a slot in one of the Sunday magazines.'

'Heaven forbid,' said Barry wryly.

Later that afternoon, Chelsea and Laura were down at Gee Whizz helping to set tables. Ginny was doing something extraordinary with some arum lilies and an armful of driftwood and Barry was darting from bistro to kitchen and back, getting redder and redder in the face and muttering, 'Tomato coulis, caramelised oranges, peppers for the piperade,' under his breath.

When they had finished folding the final table napkin, Laura gave a big yawn and flopped into the nearest chair.

'Not tired already, Laura?' asked Ginny ramming a lily into a brass urn.

'It's Charlie,' explained Laura. 'Every morning at three o'clock he yells blue murder and wakes me up. Then I just nod off and he starts again at six. You'd think modern science could invent some slow-release milk pill for babies, wouldn't you?'

'Why don't you spend the weekend at our house?' suggested Chelsea. 'She can, can't she, Mum?'

'Of course she can – why don't you pop through to the office and give your mum a call?'

'Brilliant – thanks, Mrs Gee.'

While Laura was phoning, Chelsea went through to the kitchen to see how her dad was getting on.

He was nowhere to be seen, and Chelsea strolled over

to one of the cookers and stuck her finger in a pan of sauce bubbling on the hob.

'Mmm, nice,' she murmured out loud.

'Madam is too kind!'

Chelsea jumped and turned round.

Standing before her, wielding a wooden spoon in one hand and an aubergine in the other, was the world's most drop dead gorgeous guy.

'Hi, I'm Todd. Will's nephew,' he said, dropping the aubergine and holding out a hand. 'I'm your dad's new sous-chef – well, I'm a student, actually, but sous-chef sounds more grand. My uncle tells me this is all good experience for a future hotelier!'

'Hi,' murmured Chelsea. 'I'm Chelsea – Barry's daughter.'

'Great – you going to be doing the odd spot of work here as well?' he asked, beaming at her.

'Yes, definitely,' said Chelsea, who was of the mind that she would take a short sojourn to Mars if Todd was piloting the spacecraft.

'I say, you wouldn't do me a favour, would you?' he asked. 'Just chop these mushrooms – I'm running late and your dad is a hard taskmaster!'

While she chopped, Chelsea discovered that Todd was staying with his uncle, knew no one in Leehampton and didn't have a regular girlfriend.

'You wouldn't like to come out with me tomorrow, would you?' he asked. 'Sundays are going to be my only free day. We could catch a movie,' he added.

Yes, thought Chelsea, mentally punching the air.

No, thought Chelsea, coming down to earth.

'I'm sorry,' she said, 'but I've got a mate staying for the weekend. I can't let her down.'

'OK, no sweat,' said Todd, chucking a handful of herbs into a pan. 'Another time, maybe?'

'Maybe,' said Chelsea, grinning. 'Maybe.'

The Leehampton Series

Just Don't Make a Scene, Mum!

I Think I'll Just Curl Up and Die!

How Could You Do This to Me, Mum?

Does Anyone Ever Listen? (October 2006)

Also available by Rosie Rushton
from Piccadilly Press:

Meet the girls: Holly, Tansy, Jade and Cleo.
Each book follows one week in their lives –
but what a week! Disasters, parents, secrets,
boyfriends and more challenge the girls.

Four friends. Seven days. About a hundred
things that can (and will) go wrong!

www.piccadillypress.co.uk

☆ The latest news on forthcoming books

☆ Chapter previews

☆ Author biographies

☆ Fun quizzes

☆ Reader reviews

☆ Competitions and fab prizes

☆ Book features and cool downloads

☆ And much, much more . . .

Log on and check it out!

Piccadilly Press